Welbore St. Clair Baddeley

Legend of the Death of Antar, an Eastern Romance

Also, Lyrical Poems, Songs, and Sonnets

Welbore St. Clair Baddeley

Legend of the Death of Antar, an Eastern Romance
Also, Lyrical Poems, Songs, and Sonnets

ISBN/EAN: 9783744787857

Printed in Europe, USA, Canada, Australia, Japan

Cover: Foto ©Andreas Hilbeck / pixelio.de

More available books at **www.hansebooks.com**

LEGEND OF THE DEATH

OF ANTAR,

𝔄n 𝔈astern 𝔕omance.

ALSO

LYRICAL POEMS, SONGS, AND SONNETS.

BY

WELBORE ST. CLAIR BADDELEY.

LONDON:
DAVID BOGUE, 3, ST. MARTIN'S PLACE, W.C.
1881.

CHISWICK PRESS:—CHARLES WHITTINGHAM AND CO.
TOOKS COURT, CHANCERY LANE.

TO

LOUIS FLOERSHEIM

AND

EDMUND CHRISTY.

"Take thy wings
And haste thee where the grey-eyed morne perfumes
Her rosie chariot with Sabæan spices;
Flie where the evening from th' Iberian vales
Takes on her swarthy shoulders, Heccate,
Cround with a grove of oaks."

CHAPMAN, *Bussy D'Ambois.*

LEGEND OF THE DEATH OF
ANTAR,

An Eastern Romance.

DRAMATIS PERSONÆ.

ANTAR, *a Warrior.*
JERIR, *a Warrior, brother to* ANTAR.
AMRU, *a friend to* ANTAR.
WEZAR, *a blind Archer.*
NEDIM, *a young Slave.*
ABLA, *Bride to* ANTAR.

Chorus.

ARABIA, *circ.* A.D. 450.

ANTAR.

PART I.

*A rocky place near a deep ravine, over which the early
dawn throws an increasing brilliance on the ancient
trunks of an adjacent forest. Enter a* CHORUS *of
white-robed maidens, celebrating Spring.*

CHORUS I.

Sing aloud, thou beautiful grove:
  For the days of gladness appear!
Sing sweet, thou exquisite dove :
  Breathe soft in the rose-bud's ear!
For the light of the Heaven is filled with Love,
  And the time of betrothal is near.

Far, far is the Winter's cold,
  And the days of the long decline ;

B

The flowers are abrim with the wine
Of the morn, and ablaze with its gold ;
And the undulant airs are abroad as of old,
   And the violets' odour, divine.

The songs of Sorrow have faded away ;
   Our ears are filled as with light ;
For the strain of the sun-clad herald of Day
   Is heard in the azure height :
And the Bulbul poureth his passionate lay
   Abroad on the balmy night.

And glowing afar from the sunrise, lone,
   The Angel of Love is driven ;
And flower-sweet things from her lips are blown,
   And manifold graces are given :
While Winter, aloft on his ice-girt throne,
   Is lost in the glory of Heaven.

Sing aloud, thou flowering grove :
   For the lilies of gladness appear !
Sing early and late, thou pearl-winged dove :
   Breathe soft in the rose-bud's ear !

For the breezes of Heaven are laden with Love,
    And the time of betrothal is near.

[*This chorus is heard recedingly till there enters
another group garlanded with white flowers, celebrating the marriage-day of* ANTAR *and* ABLA.

CHORUS II.

May the rose-girdled Angel of Spring scatter heavenly
    flowers in their way :

For twain Loves true arc divine, and more than married
    are they !

He bringeth her glory of heart, She giveth him joy of
    her hand :—

She Heaven's true Lady on Earth, and He, bright Lord
    of the Land.

May the forest and fadeless Field redouble the strain
    that we sing !

Not alone be this upland ravine their sweet praise
    murmuring !

For Beauty too often, God wot, is wedded to Belial,
    plain :—

Soon broken of Love and delight, and enthralled by
    the demons of Pain !

" Might seems bootless enough, and Wisdom—a queer
man's dream !"
Even so are the flowering boughs set adrift on the
passionate stream.
Yet Wisdom is lordship of gladness, and glory it is to
be Strong ;
And allied unto Beauty by Love, They make Life like
unto Song !

Another Group enters.

Who are ye ? for our senses are freshen'd to fathom
things yet without form,
Like the sheen of the Sun's breath falling aslant
through the lips of a storm !—
As a gardener fore-shadows through Winter the luck
of his April roses,
So We would fore-bode the bright fruit of their Love
ere its blossom uncloses !

First Group.

But why press darkly away from the visible paths
of our art ?

[Clouds rapidly over-spread the sky.

Second Group.

Should feeling bow down to Thought?

First Group.

Should Wisdom give way to the Heart?

(*With renewed energy.*)

What star shall be kindled in Heaven? what Joy
　　for the Earth's Embrace,

When the sun-bright glow of his passion enraptures
　　the rose of her face?

Arabia shall revel in song for the child of eternal
　　Pride :—

For the child whose smile is her own; begot of a
　　peerless bride!

　　　　　　[*A shrieking as of wild-birds.*

Second Group.

Yet truly no longer the music of morning entrances
　　our ears ;—

But a strange, sharp sound has come up, as of eager
　　encrossing of spears!

Look ye, how a throng of wild hawks enkindles in
　　midway flight,

Some steadfast, imperial bird—the shade of whose
     pinion is night !

Twice, thrice he hath sundered their midst ; whole
     hosts of the slayers are slain !

And they flutter reluctantly down to the blood-dripping
     lips of the plain.

But his innermost entrail is torn, for the pangs of his
     passion are heard :

As a meteor ascends through the sky, darts the fiery
     god-like bird !

He thunders and reels in the height, and his pride
     flutters to and fro,

Shaken darkly aloft on the wind, as through autumn
     the lost leaves go !—

Now fainting through sheer fled Life, in a storm of
     his plumes doth he fall :—

Swung round—made drunken with Death :—his foes
     for a funeral pall.

First Group.

Alas ! what dire new thing is so nearly foreshadowed
     to-day ?

Second Group.

Perchance 'tis an Augur himself, being led by a stranger
this way !

[WEZAR, *led by* NEDIM, *emerges slowly from the
forest. The* CHORUS *draw together as in inqui-
sitive dread. The sky still darkens.*

WEZAR.

The fitful notes of little forest-birds
Till now have softly fallen on my ears :
Till now, too, on my branded lids, the night
Of Day withheld, has clung inexorably !
But here the varying tints of tenderest rose
Send cheerier summons through my wistful brain :—
Songs, too, I hear—bright miracles of tune !
Nedim, whence are these strains ?

NEDIM.

For we are come
Unto the glimmering verge of this vast wood.
Beautiful girls dividing their glad lips,
Sparkle in merry dance.

WEZAR.

What stays their song ?

NEDIM.

Seeing thy sudden form emerging hence,
And girdled round with daggers : they have stilled
Their gentle music for to gaze at thee.

WEZAR.

Was it a strain of merriment or praise ?—
For since the noon was darkened from my soul
Thou know'st my ears gat craft for subtlest touch
Of sound : and sight reigns not the lord of senses,
Since I am mastered by most royal song.
Therefore, more music !   Bid them sing again.

NEDIM.

Master, they'd not sing, though a king should bid !
How then should they sing for me, a beardless slave ?—
They must have heart to sing from.

WEZAR.

Give them gold !
Thev'd sell their songs and bodies for a coin.

NEDIM.

Nay, your own eyes, good master (had you them),
Would chide the thought of that.

WEZAR.

                    Can such be found ?–
Such as forego idolatry to Him
Who swayeth most—nay, even the bard himself?
If bards be they!—but ask them of their song.

NEDIM (*advancing a little*).

The chase-stained garb, I fear, offends ye, maidens:
We would not mar your songs!

CHORUS (*laughing derisively*).

                    Thou poor, fond Slave!
Mark we—a knave of excellent chivalry!
But let us question of the man, his master!

                          [*To* NEDIM.

Who is yon man that comes from dreadful shades
Of immemorial forest, like some fiend;
And like the north wind, girt with horrid knives,—
Yet seeming blind?

WEZAR.

In sooth, this I will speak,
When ye do render me fit theme for song !
Ah, fear me not, fair maids ; I am so blind
Your Beauty's light may never pierce the veil :
I have not seen a flower for five, long years.

CHORUS.

We grudge no man a hero, or his praise !
    [They sing sonorously in hurried time to the
       music of cymbals.

As for Him, his splendour is seen in battle :—
Spears like dazzling serpents around him hissing ;
Crashing blades and thundering hoofs of chargers :
    Slayer of heroes !
On their haunches he drives the thin-flanked horses.
All the battle reels as a storm-smitten vessel,
While he, lightning-like, dashes among the foemen,—
    Lion undaunted !
Lo ! like sun-dawn over the moving waters,
Shines his fearful sword ! And like leaves of the
    Autumn,

Fall the blood-stained foes as he furrows onward :

Freer of women !

All his armour is dyed as the flower of Judas :

All the sand is aglow as with crimson blossoms ;

While he sighs on Abla, daughter of Malik,—

Maiden of maidens !

[*Then softly, with tanbour charqy.*

And for her—his beautiful, bright-eyed Abla—

In her tent she lies like an island of spices,

Fairer far than pearly-winged heavenly Houris :

Loved of the West Wind !

Her glances are as arrows of song to a Lover ;

Her mouth is sweet as a wine-filled chalice of flowers.

Her cheeks resemble the peony of the gardens :—

Lily of women !

Pleasant her lips to kiss, like the rain-lit roses ;

Raven tresses flow from her snow-white temples.

When a mortal sorrowing, gazes on her,

Rapture inflames him.

[*The echo dies.*

A SINGLE VOICE.

Antar, is His name : Abla is His bride.

WEZAR (*becoming infuriate*).

God's light !   New frenzy shudders thro' my soul !

          [*The* CHORUS *flies in all directions.*

Put me my bow.   I will play Death to them !

Now have I that same one which spake his name.

          [*He shoots an arrow that strikes a tree.*

CHORUS.

Thou fool !   A tree may bear well short of an axe !

WEZAR (*more deliberate*).

This is a shaft I will not loose in vain !

NEDIM.

Master, they shift them in such nimble-wise,

You might waste swords as sagely on their song,

As these true arrows on their safe retreat.

WEZAR.

Silence, sick fool !   Thy noise unwhets my ear !

Quickly, another shaft !

NEDIM.

        O stay your hand !

WEZAR.

Fury deprive their souls! That cursèd name!

CHORUS (*remotely*).

O thrice-skilled, vaunting, miserable fool!
Thy bearing might have made thee good report.
Not all in vain is this dull savagery:
For thou hast learned that thy much-boasted skill
Is powerless 'gainst Song. Great God above
Guards the bright children of his voice on Earth.
Prithee shame not thyself again!

NEDIM (*beseechfully*).

                Good sir!

WEZAR.

Hell's devils aid them! Nay, in Hell's despite,
I'll send this evil on them. Aha! one falls!
My wit's more pregnant than a wise man's saw!
      [*Derisive laughter, then intense silence.*

NEDIM.

A little bird was winging, tree to tree,
When thy fierce arrow strook him to the plain.
Natheless its life was brief enough!

WEZAR.

Cursed sage !

Thou hast too much of pity in thy soul
For worthy uses.

NEDIM.

Nay, then, God help thee !
Have not I wrongs like thine to be revenged ?
Did not this Antar slay the womb that bore me ?
Did he not turn the children's hair to grey,
Rushing down like the wind in Winter-time ?
But do I anger out at foolish straws,
Or wear a shapely grief to scornèd rags ?

WEZAR (*as if indifferent*).

Are those soft saints still babbling damnably ?
Sophist and slave ! I prithee once again,
Ere I be quit of thee, lead me to Him.
I will not ask thee for another mock,
Nor curse thee, will I, for thy indolence ;
But wander ever, like some meagre brook,
Laving the feet of things that give thee shade !
I will not bid thee lead me otherwise

Than this to where He camps. Yea! let us be friends!
Is not he falsest who forsakes the blind?—

NEDIM.

For feeble is the aid within themselves!
Well, too, thou know'st that when the tyrant's chains
Shed forth their bitter rust upon thy limbs,
I, only I, did tend on thy least desires,
And with my breath did ease thy smarting lids;
Nor stayed my tongue to beg new favourings,
Though at my peril!

WEZAR.
Hide thy banterings!
Is my breast hairless? Tell me—for thou knowest—
Where is the tyrant that put out these eyes?
Place unto place, and promise unto promise;
Ever delaying, with excuse replete;
Talking for deeds and shrinking from occasion,—
Thou hast now led me near him by mischance.
But this shall be the last of thy deceivings.
Yea, point the place of his soft triumphing,
That I may, as some blithe home-wending bird,

Into the long-sought nest, my full beak dip,
And greet Him, though with Death's infernal kiss,
Whom most, for doing me that cursèd sin,—
For Sin's sweet sake, I love.

NEDIM.

It is most false.
I never did deceive you.   You are thankless.

WEZAR.

Thou would'st be bribed !   It shall not be withheld.
Take thee this gold.   It is thy lawful hire.

NEDIM.

Good master, good brave master, speak not so !
Dost deem this heart loves more thy gold than thee ?

WEZAR.

Nedim, my sight is too far quenched to see !

NEDIM.

But dost thou trust to slaying Antar there ?

WEZAR.

Point me this loathly tyrant in his lair !

NEDIM.

That we shall do—may be the last we do !

WEZAR.

Then do it well : 'tis best done that's done true.

NEDIM (*as in a vision, drawing close*).

There is a green nook by a mighty stream :

   Euphrates is its name, renowned in song.

   Lithe willows lean from either bank along.

Beneath, the river glides, like one in dream ;

And on the far side doth the silver gleam

   Of happy tents illume the evening sky :

   Like little stars they glance out merrily,

And pleasaunce from each door doth sweetly beam.

Beyond it rise the giant mountains old ;

   Their great feet gird the widening plain below,

   Where wet long grasses, like soft billows, flow—

Revealing in their waves the height so cold.

There sleeps the bridegroom by his tender bride ;

   There cleave the flower-soft lips of Love this night ;

   There Antar revels in each sweet delight,

Where foes are none and Abla is his Pride.

               [*Starting in rhapsodic gestures.*

C

But my old mother's bones cry up on his soul :—
  " He hath slain me, my boy, he hath slain.
And ne'er shall I sleep in my shallow hole
  Till the tyrant beside me hath lain.
The ravens are picking my sun-dried bones,
  And an owl is perched on my head :
Thy ears shall be dinned with the noise of my groans
  Till he, my destroyer, be dead.
O, my face was fair, and my sun-bright hair
  Was the cause of my annoy ;
Now worms are knotting my cheek so fair,
  For they slaughtered me, my sweet boy."

WEZAR.

God's night !   I hear those demons yelping still !
Come, leave them to their daylight harlotries.
Hence ! away !   [*Exeunt.*

PART II.

After a day's journey.   Twilight.

NEDIM.

Master! our toil is finished.   We are come
Unto an open place anear the stream ;
And all the plain upon the further side
Is patterned out in little peaks of white ;
And where the mighty snows are gathered up
Into the lofty mountains, far above,
A liquid rose-light grandly pours itself,
Like an illumined flood of Love's sweet flowers.
And on the royal azure of high Heaven
The everlasting stars are glittering.
All seems as if God's peace reigned here supreme.
I see imperial palm-trees, whose each branch
Darkens the starlight into pearly spray
On the near tent-sides.   And cool fragrancies,

Stealing the breath with sweetness, flow along ;

And in the whirlings of the raven river

I can see golden fruits new-fallen there,

Hurried down helpless to the lips of waste.

And tiny bats are gadding up and down,

Tangling the light and dark.

WEZAR.

What sound is that ?

NEDIM.

Lo ! yonder is a tent most fair of all,

And in the garden of its snowy skirt

Feeds a slim courser, ebon as the night ;

And planted upright in the tender sod

Lightens a terrible spear.   Its glorious blade

Glimmers, like Sirius seen upon a mist ;

While, like sweet April through the darkened world,

Thitherward wind two streams of maidenhood,

Holding bright harps enwreathed with silver flowers,

Which they seem tuning.

WEZAR.

Nedim, what thou seest

Is Antar's tent ; and that proud courser there

Must be the cloudy Abjar ; that cursèd lance
Span me full thrice upon the hateful dust.
Thrice vanquished have I rolled before the feet
Of that fell charger, till my thankless tribe
Scorned me as one cast out.

> [*Lifting his head, and turning imaginarily to*
> *the camp.*

                      Ill fortune be
Upon thee, Antar! Shedad's bastard! Hell's
Sole maker of my shame! Eternal night
Clings all around me. Never in sweet sleep
Do my seared eyelids close as once they closed
In reckless boyhood. No green leaf of flower
Brightens this dismal wilderness of mine.
But now may Fortune, favouring me at last,
Cause thee to die, fierce tyrant, by this hand,
That flinched not when thy rods were simmering
Upon the windows of the world to me.
Play on thy love-wrought playings : catch the sighs
Of her, thy playmate ; sleep in her clear bosom,
Where yet thy raven locks may lie ungreyed.
Let thy words meet as music in her ears ;
Satiate thyself with joys to me denied,

Until thy despot soul is slaked of them.

For, if this little sighing breeze speak true,

There shall be echoes to its infant sob

Among these willows ; and in the breast of death

Thou wilt not find sweet lips to comfort thee,

Nor lithe white arms to mimic crushing thee ;

Nor in the gritty soil, parched-up of sun,

Wilt thou meet kisses worthy of true love.

Fill up, I say, the measure of delight :

For by the evil in man's heart, I swear

There shall be noise of tears and bitterness

Between these hours.   God's curse, I know, is
        come :

Natheless thy blood may make him purge thy sin !

For shed life felt is soothcless agony,

Whose pulsing moments mirror infinite years.

Therefore, if poison on thy boasted strength

Have masterdom, thou'lt surely grieve to Death.

Give me to drink !—my rage is choking me !—

Now lead me on a little to some spot,

Which, on thy oath, doth lie against his tent

So straightly that no shaft can fail to smite

A nestling bird, should it make crying thence.

NEDIM.

Master, I will.   The quiver here is full,
And here thy bow, already tautly strung.

[*Going aside.*

O hark! those maidens singing blissful peace!
How sweet, methinks, to be amidst them there!
Their strings do seem to catch the river's tone,
And utter its gentle spirit to these stars.
One might imagine all its depths were gold,
And sweet angelic flowers did bow their heads
From out each little fairy cloistering.
Now is there come soft trouble to their harps
Which is not in their voices: like a wind
That hurls dark waterspouts among the ships.
How will the melody long captive made   [*Pausingly.*
Sunder such hurtling bonds?   List! now it glides!
The same fair lover joins his deathless love—
But it is after life!

WEZAR.

Come on, mad boy,
Else they will hear thy maundering ecstasies.

LOTUS SONG (*from beyond*).

I.

Under her tent of glimmering leaves,
　　Bright as a pearl-white dove,
On the river's breast softly heaves
The fairy Lotus-flower, and weaves
　　Her own sweet dream of Love.

II.

And all the mighty river-song
　　Glideth round her, like a dream ;
And all the battling currents throng
To catch her Love as they eddy along :—
　　Lady of Life's sweet stream !

III.

Like a silver cloud in the clear blue day ;
　　Like a star on the azure night ;
Like a blossom aglow in the bright spring-way ;
Like a sudden joy in a life gone grey ;—
　　Is this flower of Love's delight !

IV.

When all the gay children of the fields
   Grow dim, or fall to the mower ;
The Angel of Love this bright flower shields
From the sharp red sword that the season wields,
   And endues it with power !

V.

A virtue there lives in its radiant mien,
   That maketh a broken heart whole !
On the face of a sky where no star is seen
It smiles—like Peace where battle hath been :—
   This sweet flower of the soul !

PART III.

SCENE I.—*On the further side.   Within the tent*
of ANTAR.   *Early night.*

ABLA.

Lo, Antar, on the softly-closing harps
Clouds are come up! the strain they gave, methought
Something too sorrowed, since we look for joy.

ANTAR.

The inspiration of great song is sad,
And the divinest love is not unlike :
Yet, for the bettering of our merriment,
To-morrow night let there be mirth and dances :
So, Sweet, we shall be suited.

ABLA.

     Yet, dear Love,
There was a season—ere our Absian tribe,

By many foes oppressed, gat poor and weak—
That brightest music winged our gladdest words,
And each one's heart tuned forth the general joy
(Seeing we scarce knew sorrow).   But, look you,
Since we have borne a long captivity ;—
Yet by thy mighty prowess being set free,
More than before, we now rejoice in peace,—
Our poets write us dirges and mean cares ;
And for our mirth we sing brief tragedies,
Set to the whining beauty of new harps !
Dost thou remember, Love, when first thou loved'st ?

ANTAR.

Abla, my soul, and when did I not love ?

ABLA.

And dost thou recollect a little song—
Laid by Love's fingers down amid the flowers
That sparkled round my tent at Jelilel ?—

ANTAR.

Yea, love ; yet cannot I call back the lines :
My soul hath since been uttered more by spears
Than through the wooing veils of modest song.

ABLA.

My maidens wrought for it this dainty frame,
And they have learned it ; aye, it shall be sung.

[*Sung from without.*

SONG.

I.

Thy maidens are but as wild-flowers sweet ;
　　But thou art as Love's bud-ròse,
Whose passionate lips of their own sweet, meet
　　When the wings of the night unclose !
　　No virtue untold that the violet knows,
Nor the treasure of no white garland, I weet,
　　May dare to emulate those.

II.

The kiss in my dream that I took from thee
　　A vision of Paradise weaves ;
Though still, like a summer-lit stormy sea,
　　My passion within me heaves !
　　And the clasp that I gave,—ah ! still it deceives !
For like the lithe branch of a Tamarisk-tree,
Was thy shape as I gathered its beauty to me,—
　　As the wave of the branch with its leaves.

III.

I lifted away thy fragrant veil,
   O Abla, thou fairest-born!
Thy breath was as soft as the Syrian gale,
   And thy face—it was like the morn!
   And ah! with thy smile, my bosom forlorn,
Like soft air smitten with furious hail,—
Like the voice of the amorous nightingale,
   By the demon of rapture was torn!

                      [A great barking of dogs.

ANTAR (*rising*).

The watch-dogs bay! Some keen-lipped pard perchance,—
They are not wont to bay so suddenly.

ABLA (*entreatingly*).

O go not forth these arms for so slight cause,—
Lest my lament go too, to cry thee back!

                      [She restrains him.

Prithee, O my sweet Lord, those dogs do bay
Upon each night with communing the moon;
Who doth put on from her own mystic light,

Uneven visage and fantastic shape,

To work upon their fond unreasoned minds.

They will not cease, I think, though one should pray.

ANTAR.

Nay, Love, but let me go forth ; nor for Love's sake

Forget the perils that may lurk around :

> [*Softlier to her.*

For there are foes beneath night's sable wing

As there are Loves and Angels.

ABLA.

> Yet, sweet Love,

Should foes affright us,—angels being at hand ?

I do bethink me I have sometime heard

That dolorous music gives a sort of woe

Unto the fixed attent of kindly brutes :

And for this, too, the watch-dogs bay so loud.

Hark how the sound has travelled !

ANTAR.

> O most dear Love,

You do persuade me while you most restrain.

I shall be back ere thou canst say, "He's gone!"
For well thou know'st how Pleasure, cut in twain,—
Doth knit its parts more firmly than before!

[He goes out.

ABLA.

And is he gone,—and Abla could not stay him?—
Let me look forth! The moon is wandering far
Behind a tawny continent of clouds.
Night on her velvet wings has issued forth
And darkened out the bright engrailèd stars.
The night-bird sings not any more! I ween
It is a season fits nor friend nor foe.
Save would foes come beneath confusion's flag,
And perish of themselves. But yond I see
One bright almighty beam between the clouds:
It falls like—Ah! what cry is that?—He calls!

[She listens.

ANTAR (*from without, faintly*).

Ah me! and in the darkness!

ABLA.

Why! he speaks
As if he did regret the night had come!

[She goes out of the tent.

ANTAR (*by the river*).

Out, thou slim thief!—There; let it be thy shame,
Base, perjured shaft, to grovel on the plain !
Though thy smooth lineaments do woo the air
To soar and there outvie in winged speed
The royal lightning's self.   And thou out there,—
Whose dastard fingers tuned them at my voice ;—
Who thought'st to triumph o'er my heedless ways :
Would that mine eyes might cleave this night to thee !
That I might wither with a brave man's smile
And shrink thy craven limbs—a most fit feast
For the rank carrion-fowls that led thee here.
Was the high sun too scornful of thy deeds ?
Would not the patient moon admit thy prayer ?—
(Loathing too much to be enleagued with Hell)
That thou most fulsome traitor, from that hole
Hast made a covenant with hindering night
To smite me here ?—not as a valiant foe
Who might outface an hundred made like thee,
In the just noon,—his back against his heart,—
But me a weaponless, unreckoning man !
Yet think not thus to 'scape my sure revenge !

There is yet power in openness alone
Which can upfill the level of its wrong.

        [A heavy groan is heard from beyond.

Enter JERIR *and others; then* ABLA.

JERIR.

Brother, what ails thee ?

ABLA.

        Ah ! why speaks he thus ?

ANTAR.

Abla, art thou here ?

ABLA.

        For I heard your voice.

ANTAR.

Some subtle reptile sneaking in yon reeds
Hath set his paltry fang upon my thigh !
Help me a little : the wound hath been so swift
That it forgets to bleed.

D

JERIR.

I will set eyes—nay! flame this sooty steel
In the fell traitor's blood.

[*He plunges into the river.* ANTAR *is helped
to his tent.*

SCENE II.

ANTAR (*within the tent*).

Look not so grave, sweet friends, on this my hurt :
There is no need Despair!   Yet, to you all,
Let me now note how strangely Fortune doeth ;
Who, through unnumbered fights and often peril,
E'en to the lips of danger, held me scatheless ;
As if the battling airs were impotent
While I stood by : yet do behold how here,
A single shaft she has let pass at me,
Not as it were, upon the visible day,
Wherein a nice consideration aims,
And fools itself in error ;—but, alas!
Under the hopeless raven-wing of night ;
Where it meseems my voice became the targe,
And I do fear was smitten.

AMRU.

                     An 'twere thy life

We swear revenge upon this devilish deed!

Methinks the noble Jerir comes apace.

                           [*Enter* JERIR.

ANTAR.

What fortune guided thee, O valiant one?

JERIR.

Most noble brother, proof is here—without!

When, after a fond battle with the stream

(Whereon the darkness seemed so thickly packed

It clung about my face till I scarce knew

Whether the stream or it most made me strive),

I took the sandy bank and loitered out—

Scarce one spare pace on dry land had I gone—

When, as a wanderer in some fern-grown wood

Stumbles perchance upon some hidden log

Felled in the winter, but still unremoved,—

I tripped, as I first deemed, on sleeping beasts;

But with my outstretched hands I felt a man!

I found no wound on him.   But like some pine

That fiery storms have smitten, he lay there,

In mixed caparisons of chase and war ;
And thus, by many bafflings, am I here.
Behold : 'neath yonder cere-cloth, there now lies
This poor slain man !

> [*They bring in the corpse and uncover it.*

ABLA.

Alas ! why doth he start so ?—
In outward quiet, seem so inly raving ?

ANTAR.

O, Abla, sweet ! O heaven forgive my soul !

> [*Restraining himself.*

ABLA.

My dearest Lord, why speak you to me so ?
I cannot bear to gaze upon that face !
It is so wild with Death ! When I see Death,
O may I see it in that soft serene,
As if the gentle spirit that doth seem
To smile delighted through the stilled distress
Of the beloved, were floating in my sight!
But oh, my Lord, as you now gaze at me,
Meseems you steal the iciness of Death
From that dread visage !

ANTAR.

Abla, O my dove,
Whose love to me was as my morning-star,
In whose most heavenly resplendency
Life's fierce reverses have been duly fought
And I have vanquished them :—O, most dear Love,
I would not speak so bitter-sweet a word
To one so loved ; but Love itself conspires
And forces me through my preventing will
To quench in thee Hope's all-inspiring flame !
That is the corpse of Wezar, son of Carad,
Whose venomous spite, behold, thus comes abroad
In his last shaft.   Of foes the fatallest !
Among all mine, the sole one feared of me ;
Though most within my power !

ABLA.

Is that the same ?

ANTAR.

Thrice at my feet he crouched down in the dust,
Wrested from off his horse ; and all those times
I gave him back the freedom he had lost :
For he was brave, and splendid in assault ;

And when he shouted, warriors fled before him :—
Where he struck he cleft ; where, too, he thrust, de-
      stroyed.
Yet, like a craven, envious of just Fame—
Ungrateful for the Freedom that he swayed
From my good-will—three several times he tried
With his own hand to murder me outright!
Twice I forgave him for the same old cause:
For he was brave in battle!   What I spared,
Was one small hero-part.   But inasmuch
As, saving that, he was a murderer,—
Hateful in God's eyes, and a curse to men,—
I did command that those two guilty orbs,
Which, as two evil planets, led him on
To things most dastardly, should be put out.
And so he came by those poor blearèd lids,
And they retold me,—they who did the deed,—
What demon ravined there within the man :
For, when but quit those dreadful torturers
That brought him darkness on this side the grave,
He cursed my soul, and laughed out blasphemies ;
Rheuming upon their faces.   This wretch thought
To live—nay, flourish ! on my fair perdition—

To make my death a spring-song for his soul ;
But Death hath ta'en him too.   We should rejoice
If but a twinkling we outlive a foe :—
For his off-taking proveth Death our friend !

ABLA.

But who, sweet Lord, puts Hope thus far from You ?
To whom with me, not one brief hour ago
She was a dear divideless friend ?   Alas !
Does a mere shaft-wound thus unmettle you :
A little harmless flower of a wound ?—
You, who in Danger's brunt deride the lance
Lifted to kill—the steely terrible sword ?
How puny is this hurt !   I do not think
But ere to-morrow's eve it will be closed.

ANTAR.

Yea ! closed with a little stanching, yellow sand ;
To keep Death in her new-found Dwelling-place,
And lock her from my friends !   O my true Love,
E'en thus I fall the wings of all my hopes,
And droop the pinions of my soaring Love ;—
And on the golden morning-time to come,

I'll fold the plumes of courage to their rest.
That shaft was dipped in Death. Gaze once again,
Upon that vengeful mass of infamy !
Mark you the curses of that tortured lip :—
The fettered mischief of that lowering brow,
Where silent thunder ruins :—the very ear
Bemocks with daintiness each virtuous sound.
Did not the clouds come up upon our singing ?
So will Death come, my Sweet, my only Love,
Upon the matins of the little birds !
I see her sable train within the breeze !—
The wind of Life drives back their darkling robes,
But there's no question on her bloodless lips,
And they advance her scutcheon steadfastly.
Her eyes are bright imperial to me !—
Abla, methinks, like thine. And in her mouth
I see a bud-rose blanched—a fading pleasure !—

        [ABLA *folds her arms around him.*

A maiden's love-song !—Aye ; it is as white
As those fair hawthorn flowers around my neck !—

   *   *   *   *   *   *

Then, when she saw his thoughts were wandering,
And he spake less with reason than with dreams,

Abla, calling aloud in utter grief,
Dewed her beautiful garments with her tears ;
And her fair cheeks, like lilies of the garden,
Shone with the moving sorrow.   For in her heart,
She saw herself led forth as bride to Death :
And wondered much that Fate should use her so.
But when his words were known among the tents,
Sounds of dull grief went o'er the cloudy night ;
And noise of grieving women filled the Dark ;
Soiling their perfumed hair with loathly dust—
Tearing their raiment.   But the Child of Malik,
Thinking upon the sorrows of her tribe,
Burst into passionate woe beside her spouse :—

" O Race of Abs ! thy glory is gone for ever !
Dark too are all thy Days : for thy sun is fallen !
Souls illustrious, weep for the matchless hero—
                Lionous Antar.

" Heaven is dark ! the light of his sword is faded !
All our foes drank death at his hands like water !
Lakes of wine made He for the lapping lions :
                Slaying the tyrants !

" Ah ! but his Love was sweeter to me than honey !
Lovelier far than roses are to the friendless !
Loyaller He than the best of the race of mortals :
            Nobler in counsel !

" All our people gloried that I was happy ;
Sang their songs rejoicing at this our wedding ;
Knew not I should have, ere the day was ended,
            Death for a bridegroom !

" Down the darkness, in the terrible silence,
Lonely saw I luminous eyes that loved me :—
Saw the straining throat and the god-like temples
            Gleam through the blackness.

" Heard his splendid voice in its powerful anguish
Open sweetly, hovering o'er my senses,
Winged with Deathless Love :—Ah ! who shall comfort
            Heart-stricken Abla ? "

PART IV.

As when, upon some latter Autumn night,
Made sultry by the long-stored summer heat,
A mighty river of cloud pours down between
The desolate jagged heights that girdle in
Fragrant-islanded Oorah, dark and calm,—
Out of the mystic stillness breaks a flash,
Full in tremendous glory, like a thread
Darted from off the shuttle of our Fate,
Or as a chink that shews Eternity;
And after one sharp hurtling crack, the thunder
Swells into awful breves among the peaks
And gold-grey gorges winding far away,
Forgotten of water;—so, within that camp,
From that bright dwelling, thiswise went Grief abroad.
And all the live-long night new sounds of woe
Gathered under the dark unpitying clouds,
Where the craped moon stole swiftly. But when morn,

Mounting in dazzling armour on the heights,
Like some bold warrior, scared the wolvish mists,—
Antar, yearning amid fell agonies,
Spake to his weeping friends :—" Let no more tears,
O valiant, well-loved comrades, dim your eyes!
Under the self-same law God sways us all!
Who may withdraw himself from destiny?"
Then, leaning softly round to Abla, said :—
" Belovèd spouse.   Alas! I being dead,
Who shall defend thine honour and thy life?
Well know I that the tribe of Banu-Abs,
Stricken of this my strength, and these my arms,
Will surely be o'erwhelmed.   The whole land cries
For vengeance on it.   Yea! none but as me
Can save you from the pangs of slavery.
Amer and Zeid-el-Khail alone of all,—
Of all the warriors who wear horse-tail helms,—
Who fought by us at sandy Jelilel,
Can now defend your honour and your tribe!
Choose then, of these.   Yea! offer him your hand.
And, for to pass the desert safelier,—
To gain your kinsmen, thus I counsel you:
Mount Abjar, my dark courser; and in my Arms

Let your fair self be clad!   Dread no attack.

Bear yourself as beseems.   Deign no salute.

For the sight of the steed of Shedad's son,

His fadeless armour, and his terrible spear,

Will daunt the boldest."

                    Then the mighty sun

Poured his bright armies down the silver slopes

Of fair Katraneh ; and delicious breaths

Of gentle flowers that wakened from their sleep

Wandered around him there within the tent :—

Fragrance, that like old friends, recalls old scenes !

But which, alas! he scarce shall feel again.

  So, at his will, they carried him without,

Where he might breathe and see the boundless scene.

And there he gave his wealth in flocks and herds,

With all his late-won booties, to his friends :

To Abla most of all.   He gave her gems—

Beryls and topaz from the Javan isles :

Pearls that had glistered on the dusky breasts

Of far South queens ; and things of carven gold,

Wherein whole leaves of radiant emerald

Pictured the summer ; and bright silken veils,

And soft Sidonian tunics, flower-enwrought,
And curious linens of antique device,
And many-coloured scarves and spices rare,
And costly ivories and singing shells,
And things of sandal wood and cedar things,—
For he was princely, and he loved her much.

But Abla knew not, though she heard him speak.
Deep night had fastened on her wondering lids,
And like a Lady in dream with sorrowed heart
She stood ; and stanchless all her bright tears came,
Gleaming her pearlen cheeks and lashes dark,
That lightened back her soul's light.
                                         Then, more soft,
Turning to Amru, his beloved friend :—
" Amru, my soul's best friend, most loved of men !
O youth, in whom the world should take delight !
I prithee get thee back to Aneyzeh,
Fragrant, with many wells : where all thy tribe
Shine in their white pavilions like the stars.
Speak not my parting : tell no man of it.
But sometimes, when the morning breezes flow,
And all the breathing beauty of the Spring
Fireth the passionate springs about thine heart,

Then, Amru, call perchance this face to mind :
And all the tender thoughts of glorious flower,
That wedded our two souls in peace or war !
Think not of me as of one who 'neath the soil
Lies in deforming change :—a work less cared-for
By God who rules, than by the sensual worm
That garners nothing, but degrades and spoils
The pride of Nature.   But think thou of me,
As of one who never smote an helpless foe :—
As of one who, though revengeful of great wrongs,
Never in absence stung another's name ;
Nor ever did defame a noble deed ;
But rather loved to make his foe a friend ! "

Then He embraced him ; and in silence deep,
Amru, with hidden eyes, went faltering forth ;
And the sweet breezes caught his long black curls.
Thus, passing to his courser with a sigh,—
One manful groan—heard but of few besides,—
His Morning-star sped westward like the wind ;
And he was seen no more.
                              Then, through a line
Of mounted warriors glittering with straight spears,
Abla, in all the armour of her spouse,—

Fair as the moon upon the sapphire heaven,—
Came slowly, sitting astride that ebon steed.
In her glaved hand she kept the dreaded lance,
That shone like Sirius or Canopus' light,
Or the calm planet lit with many moons:
And at her side hung down the heavy sword
That crafty smiths had wrought in Samarcand.
So, to the litter that She used of old,
The trusty slaves bore Antar: and he smiled.

PART V.

As when upon some June-day by the sea,
With never a least white flake of hovering cloud
To darken the lit flowers along our path,
On the horizon a soft argent line,
Like distant visionary cliffs, is seen
Gliding unevenly, but surely on ;—
So, having lost the emerald river-banks,
Along the gold-enrippled sands are seen
Camels and driven herds and laden beasts,
And serried spears that glimmer over them :
And in their midst, like some cloud-ruling goddess
Shining in splendid state imperial,
On the dark courser, sombre-sleek as night,
Went Abla : And before her Jerir went.
And in the sumptuous litter, camel-borne,
Lay Antar, dreaming deathwards as he slept.
  But lo! upon the shimmering far verge,

E

Bordering the azure canopy of Heaven,
Myriads of tents, at first unseen of them,
Broke the wide solitude—A nest of Lions!—
And like the van-cloud of an hurricane,
An hundred horsemen, rapid as gazelles,
Hurried between the mystic desert-line
To nigh three lance-throws of the cavalcade.
Then reining short his steed, the foremost cried :—
"Antar, it is. Alas! Behold his arms ;
And Abla's gorgeous litter ; and his steed!
Let us in haste to our tents. Alas, to-day!
His wrath will be upon us : let us flee!"—
And so they turned and fled. But one old Sheik,
Well-learned in sifting signs of mystery,
Rallied some round again, and spake these words :—
"Friends, it is Antar's lance, his sword, his helm ;
His wondrous courser, coloured like the night,
But that is not his stature nor his mien.
Surely some wound or perilous malady
Prevents his mounting!—Nay,—it may be thus :
He lies within yon litter, cold and stiff ;—
And Abjar carries for disguise his spouse,
Clothed in his glittering arms." But none of them

Dared to press near : but followed from afar,

Like craven vultures scared by dying prey,

Hoping some tokens of the truth to see.

But like an early rose that Frost enjoys

Sat Abla, weak and pale for sleeplessness ;

And as the mid-day sun shot fiercelier,

Turning to liquid flame the level plain,

The mighty lance bore down her delicate arm,

And as she rode, it furrowed in the sand.

Then, as a falcon on its vantage-rock

Searches with eager reason the least spot

That moves within her still, encircling realm ;—

So with his practised eyes, that hoary Sheik,

Seeing that lance thus trailing on the sand,

Reasoned assurance to his wavering friends.

A sudden sign ! and like a shoreward wave,

Lowering their spears, they rushed upon the line.

But, like a lion's roar that fills the pause

Made by the chatter of apes and jungle-birds,

Or the boom of sea-caves that a billow strikes—

Awaking 'mid shrill cries and thud of hoofs,

And bellowing foemen, and the clang of arms,

Antar, uprising, gave a mighty shout.

And lifting up his wild, wide, blood-shot eyes,
He turned and looked : And as he looked, they fled—
Fled, clinging close along their hurtling steeds,
And vanished in a storm of whirling sand,
Shrieking aloud in terror: "Evil day!"
"Antar yet lives, and lures us with a bait
That he may try what clan will dare him most."
So, in despite that bony-cheeked old man,
Whose subtle hints had hailed them to attack—
Despite entreaties, promises, rewards,
They fled, like silly hares that men surprise.
Yet He cried out and taunted, toiled, and cursed,
Dubbing them lustless eunuchs, till some turned.
Then halting 'mid some thirty sweltering jades,
Whose whitened flanks heaved like the foamy crests
That laugh against the ribs of dusky ships,
He begged them pry along the wilderness
And watch those winding files.   "Forsooth," said he,
" Antar is gravely wounded ; or some hurt
Having befallen him, he woos repose.
Let us then follow and take note of him !"

But Antar,—though the terrible fires of pain

Burned on relentlessly, and gave no peace,—
Bade them bring back his arms that Abla wore.
So they unlaced the helmet from her head,
And loosed the steely plates that bound her breast,
And took the heavy lance and iron glaves,
And laid her, trembling with affright and toil,
In the soft glittering litter as he rose.

Thus in his royal armour he arrayed,
And slowly faltered to caress his steed
That smote its dark hoofs in the golden sand.
But some that loved him, nearing him, spake thus :—
" Antar, for us thou hast fought well and long !
To-day then, truly, we will fight for thee !
Prithee, treasure thy yet-remaining strength,
Nor rashly cast it from thee at one throw ! "

But Antar said : " Dear friends, I hear your words ;
Yet if, in truth, I have done deeds for you,
Advance : I will defend you to the last ;
And ere to-night we shall repose in peace.
Antar still watches you ; though these, his words,
Will soon be folded in death-enwoven dreams ! "
And so they went in silence, and obeyed.

PART VI.

The Angel evening, on her glittering wings,
Stole sparkling, robed with stars, upon the east ;
The desert heard no sound, save passing flocks
And dull uneven thrum of marching steeds,
That made the sand like mill-streams eddying ;
And the new-moon, boatwise there in the twilight,
Looked on the armour that the hero wore,
And flashed betimes adown his shaken spear ;
And sometimes fired across his frosting eyes.
And softly along there roamed a humming breeze
Laden with balmy virtue from all flowers
That breathe of gladness. In the neighbouring vale,—
As when some love-gale mars a splendid rose,
And streams its crimson treasury on the air,—
The Bulbul poured his notes of sweetest woe ;
And tuberose unveiled her virgin limbs,
And sighed her regal beauty to the night.

Falling afar, soft torrents, murmuring,
Soothed eager ears—those homeward crystal streams
That wander down the Vale of Antelopes.

   Then as they came before that narrow gorge,
Antar made all the herds to pass therein.
But Abla slept : nor would he break her sleeping ;
But waved one sighing kiss above her lips,
And bade them bear her softly down the vale,
And lull her with the music that she loved.
So when they faded, and he saw no more,
And only distant dirges caught his ear ;
He turned his courser, and stayed shining there,
Like some white seaward rock that sailors fear.

   Therefore those lithe leopards that followed him
Stood marvelling aloof what he would do.—
" Let us escape beneath the sheltering night ;
For He but purposeth to destroy us all !"
But in deviceful accents that old man :—
" He has no soul who counsels infamous fear.
This movelessness, I ween, is Death's own sleep !
Natheless he is now dead ? Knew you his ways ?
Did he e'er wait the onslaught of a foe ?

Did he not glean the horsemen as men glean corn ?
He like an eagle would since have dropped on us,
And plucked the pluméd armour from our limbs !
Onward then, boldly : or at least remain
Till dawn resolve us an it be not true !"

So all that night they waited sleeplessly,
Till splendouring morn arose on purple wings,
And swept like lightning down along the hills :
Smote into glory all the hero's arms,
And sable Abjar 'neath his bright dead Lord.

Thus, like a pack of lean and agued wolves,
Sneaking around a lion as he preys,
Eyeing the carcase timidly from afar,
These prowlers stood, and shook like aspen leaves.
But their old leader, tendering no more words,
Softly took foot, and, couching his thin spear,
Circled with stealthy strides that gentle steed ;
Then, creeping snakewise, pricked him suddenly ;
And Abjar, with one mighty, fiery leap,
Darkened over the desert, letting fall
His matchless master on the sparkling sand :
And all the armour rang among the hills.

Then they all ran with one accord to him ;
Gaping amazedly, for want of words.
For he, at whom Arabia trembled, lay
Stiff, cold, and vast, along the troubled sand.
And long they gazed, and lauded his peerless
      shape :
His raven locks, all dewy in the breeze :
The burnt brow, full of counsel and command,
And tender temples of still tenderer eyes,
That yet seemed frowning proudly under Death.
And while they gazed, on wide imperial wings,
An eagle wheeled around them, and fled on.

So they bore-off his armour, taking his lance ;
But honouring a foe so justly famed,
Hollowed some sand, and laid him to his rest.
And when they stood apart, that hoary chief
Knelt down beside him, glimmering with tears :
Saying : " All honour, Hero, be to Thee :
Living, the best protector of the wronged ;
And in thy end their true defender still !
May kindly dews refresh this shallow sod
Where we, the sons of Irak, lay thee down ;

Erst foes, now friends. Sweet peace be unto
    Thee!"
There then he rests: and they all sought their
    tents.

THE END.

LYRICAL POEMS, SONGS, AND SONNETS.

LYRICAL POEMS, SONGS, AND SONNETS.

A FRAGMENT,

BEING A DREAM OF THE BIRTH OF SONG.

WITH many questionings I softly gained
How the first Poets pressed Her fervent lips ;—
Hearts full of sunrise—how the dumb brown birds
Slept not for sudden singing.   How the light
Fluttered with roses scattered from the Gods ;
And heavenly harp-strings smitten of hands unseen,—
Waxing and waning on pure passionate ears,—
Broke into strophied song, unheard before :
Felt like the soul's fire, through the golden earth,
Vocal with ecstasy !—Yea, from east to west,
Flashed as a beacon from her flower-bright heights

Over her full fair girdling atmosphere,
Waking from cloud-laden dreams. O mighty mother,
O Earth, my mother, out of thy dark, still prison,
Poised in Time's deep shadow, then wast thou loosed !
The jarring chains that rusted on thy limbs
In the eternal, ever-dripping dews,
Lifted from off thee, hearing those bright chords.
Winter was gone : Spring rose upon thy soul.
Out of the twilight Song awakened thy wings :—
Never to fold, save in delightful sleep,
While man has heart to feel and breathe and see.
I heard the Angel of Freedom cry aloud,
Above the stir of viols and bright harps :
" There is no Death henceforth."—And in my sight
A vision of grey Death, with eyes alarmed,
Slunk into soundless night for evermore.
He had no heart to curse—no hope to dream ;
But where he trode, even on the bordering air
Of thy sweet realm, blithe flowering dynasties
Revelled, like fiery foam, upon the deep,
And laughed with Life and Song. And through the
      space
A million rainbows of a myriad hues

Bound lovingly the intervolving stars,
That are the jewels on the gates of Song.
And there were wings upon the cloudless air
That made not shadows, but resplendent hues,
Like the soft harmonies beneath a song,
Where the notes kiss each other and fade by
In faint recovering passion.   Then, a voice
Soft as the Spring-tide on a windless stream,
Bade Silence die.   And in the way of Death
Silence went forth and sank for evermore.
Then all the sudden sea leapt into light,
And golden flowers of flame and silver foam
Danced in the splendour of Elysian day.
And all the streams that water the wide earth
Shone with a moving song.   And from the lips
Of joyless mortals grew a glad acclaim,
Breathing-in exultation from that scene.
And all the blue-eyed spirits of the deep
Tendered dark sapphires from their treasuries,
On the mild mistless shores.   Far over sea,
Where the wild waves kist out the willing sky,
I saw their numberless plumes, like southern birds
Meeting the April of our water-ways ;—

Armies of singing wings; and in their fingers
Each of them held a small white flower of pearl,
And all their myriad voices sang this song :—

I.

" We have slept the blind life of the sea
　In the depths of the tremulous Earth ;
Though God, who has caused us to be,
　Made us fair in the day of our birth.
We have dwelt through a dreamful sleep ;
　We slept an eternal night ;
Till we heard Song call through the deep,
　And we rose to the light.

II.

" We rose from our azure caves
　Like stars from the twilight heaven :
We sundered the sea as the waves
　In the Spring are by sea-swallows riven.
We saw all dim faint flowers
　Take life ; and the colour of death,
That had lain on their dreaming hours,
　Took flight at Light's breath.

III.

" And the streams of the sea that are fleet
   Took voice as they lightened along,
Till the chorus of things grew sweet
   With the glory of jubilant song.
And the gems of the deep sea shone
   Like the lights that in heaven appear,
For the curtain of darkness gone,
   And the splendour of Life made clear."

Then from the mouths of all the morning stars,
Winged with supreme, unutterable peace,
Came the Creation's hymn (in old time heard
By all the sons of God). But thou, O Earth,
Now heard'st that sweet, unfathomable song,
And all thy golden fields took fresh delight,
And billowed in delicious symphony.
I saw the glittering tears of gladness rise
Like sunlit springs within the summer rose
Shaken with that strange music: down its stem
Trickled reluctant fire, involuntary—
So softly ruled by song was that sweet flower
And all its balmy life fled faintly abroad,

F

Dealing rare ecstasy, unfelt before.
And like a seraph's lamp, the lily glowed,
Too bright for silver, and too pale for gold.
And on the raven pools, unproved of wind,
Like sunrise, opened wild, white water-flowers;
Swelling with rapture all unknown before;
Vision of virginhood.   The tuberose
With fragrant lips entranced the trembling air,
Breathing immortal bliss; and like the stars
Shot through an August evening, 'mid the trees
Burst the restraintless orchid.   From its heart
Swiftly some bird drew out the honeyed life,
And left it leaning, naked, slaked, asleep—
So hungered with that hymn.   For high desire,
Dreadless of ill, first set all things aflame.
Beauty was Empress; Song, her peerless son;
And all creation listened at his feet;—
His to sway: and in him there was no Sin.

FLOWER-LAND BY THE SEA.

COME to the steepy woods that be,
Thronèd by the summer sea !
We will feel the breezes flow,
As through the haggard oaks they go,
Weaving light amid the leaves,
Like the far-down wave that heaves.
Hark ! I hear its soft delight !—
Now the dark octave, in its might,
Thunders out the sussuration
With its glorious undulation :
And I see cloud-shadows flying :
  Some, like fluttered legions flee ;
Some, like purple mantles lying
  On Jehovah's jasper sea.

At our feet in the tangled gloom,
Many beauteous flowers bloom :
Foxglove, where the wild bee dwells,
Like an instrument of bells ;
In its cups there may you seek
Freckles snatched from Mary's cheek,

When she chided the young sun
For freaking her complexion.
Round the oak-tree, bowed and bent,—
Its honeyed udders full distent,—
Soft honeysuckle's twiny length
    Weaves a dainty web that mocks
    The fadeless flourish of his locks,
That speak his unabated strength.

Here, too, let no bright eye o'erpass,
Making red twilight in the grass—
Itself half-shrouded from the eye—
The goblin's supper-strawberry;
Or sweet unvarying violet,—
Like Beauty's eye oft hung with wet;—
For whom the forest wildly rings
With impassioned echoings;
Where nightingale and turtle-dove
Lead the Elfin-court of Love.
Mark, too, that little flower of Light—
    Chaster than a Lover's sonnet—
Garlanded with blades of white,
    That stills the day with gazing on it!

And note, dear friend, just over me,

This lichen-bearded apple-tree ;

And right within its shade of care,

Myriads reeling through the air.

And all around, where'er we turn,

    Gaily greeting you and me,

See the fountainous bright fern

    Floating beautiful and free !

There, too, is dock and stinging-nettle

(Which doth merely courage mettle) ;

And agaric's soft handsome snare,

And deadly nightshade groweth there.

Yes ! amid this gleam and gloom

Many beauteous flowers bloom :

Some are fair and some are duller,—

Every flower hath not gay colour,

    Nor every herb a dainty smell ;

But some of all delights are fuller—

    Odour and hue and form as well.

NEW INN, CLOVELLY,
    July, 1880.

LAMENT OF THE PEOPLE OF MALAGA.

MALAGA! Malaga!
Beautiful! lofty!
Matchless!—our mother!
Who can behold thee
Humbled and broken,
A prize to the spoiler,
And burst not to bitter
Tears in his anguish?
Where are thy castles—
Those white, high towers?—
Thy shining bulwarks
Are wasted—are fallen;
And we thy children—
Behold—we are driven
Tamely, like lions
Caught in the snaring
Net of the hunter;—
Dragging to bondage.
Far from the smiling

Hearths of our fathers,
And from thee, our mother,
Thy flowers and fountains—
To languish in darkness!

Malaga! Malaga!
What shall become of us,—
We thy grey-beards?
Thy matrons henceforward
Are held not in honour;
The nights of their glory
Are starless for ever!
Thy rose-lipped maidens,
Thy lily-like mothers,
A prey for the hated
Lust of the stranger,
Shall harden their fingers
At menial toilings:
While their lamenting
Shall be for derision,—
Yea! for the triumph
Of these thy destroyers!
Malaga! Malaga!

A VISION of ANGER and of LOVE.

" Ira surgit inter ignes."

I.

" I, ANGER, born with scorn of Sleep,
　Bear hate to the children I feed :
I fly in the track of the tears they weep,
　And drink of the drops they bleed.
I see myself rise in their lips,—in their eyes :
Their bright brows ruffle : their clear voice cries :
They roar at their victim, and when he dies,—

　　　In sweet, soft laughter,

　　　Like joy that comes after

　　　　The flood of a woman's sighs,—

　　　I pierce their hearts,

　　　And smile at their smarts :

　　　　For joy is my grim disguise.

II.

" In the sea of Hope I have hastened a wreck :
　(Old mariners laugh at my freaks :

Though, natheless, I wish all the world had one neck,
   And I heard not its dying shrieks.)
I shed warm showers of blood on the flowers ;
They fainted away in their budding hours :
I did them to death in their spring-time powers :—
     I made them to wed
     When passion was dead !
      Like swallows born after the summer,
     They shivered to Death
     In the keen white breath
      Of Winter,—Lust's after-comer ! "

" Amor surgit inter flores."

III.

" But I, LOVE, born with a scorn of Wrath,
   Though I breathe of the burning South,—
   I would the world had but one heart, and one mouth,
That my lips might kiss it forth.
I would sing to it, cling to it, girdle it round
With glad close roses and cloyless sound ;
Yea ! clothe it with sweet soft raiment of flowers,
And fold it around with radiant hours.

And in its eyes for ever should dwell

A deathless smile : a spiritual spell.

No dreadless Tempest should turn or divide

My sun-bright dream at my sweet Love's side.

I would wake with it, wanton and close with it fast :

Thus were we at first : thus shall it be, last.

    Yea ! nothing for ever

    Our lives shall dissever :

Nor shall there be grief or regret for the past."

HOMEWARDS.

OUT of the sunlit sapphire sea,
   Thy silver-columned cliffs arise :
   Love's brightest splendour in my eyes
Is not so bright as this of Thee.
Thy snowy sea-bird seems to greet.
   Small autumn-clouds to the southward flee :
   O what loved scene on Earth can be
As the loved scene I view, so sweet ?
Long have I lived in soft surmise
   That more delights in thee do meet,
   In beauties more art thou replete
Than lands more blessed with bluer skies !
Tho', when I left, no passionate heat
   Did make me feel thy Devotee :
   Now that I once more gaze on thee,
O how my heart doth fondly beat !

A VISION OF THE DEATH OF BION THE POET.

I.

BION is dead! O Sappho from thy sleep
In the Leucadian deep,
Arise and wreathe thy arms around his brows.
 Stretch thy warm self upon him till thy mouth
 Filled of his own fair south
Kiss up fled fires. Oh may thy lips arouse
 Those redolent rare flowers
That dream through the veil of death!
Ah let thy venturous breath
 Fill sweet the fearful hours!
Sappho! O Sappho, thy passion shall not fail
Thou who hast lit his living soul; all Hail!

II.

Kiss his bright limbs. O cover him with love!
 Scatter thy song about his dainty ears.
He is beside thee: thou art above;
 And one alone hears

Thy mouth like a dove,
　　Murmur between thy kissing.
Tell me my tears are sweet!
　　Clasp him close to thee!—
His lips of their own sweet, meet;
　　But move not for thee nor for me.

III.

I see thy bosom bare and bright
　　As a sea-risen star;
Thy soft wet flanks are shining white,
　　And thy feet unsandalled are.
Bion is dead! Do the leaves lie still on their boughs?
　　Bion is dead! His clear sweet eyes
Are blinded with Death's black tresses: his turned
　　bright brows
　　Lighten there through the shade where he lies.
Sever the air, sad birds, with your short shrill cries:
Death is made mad with desire, and will not let him
　　arise.

IV.

O Sappho! my sweet Sappho—art thou mute?
　　Hath the sea's mighty music quenched thy song?

Though thy quick-coming tears leap swiftly
    along,
Like broken roses of sound from the lute,
Sorrowed and strewn ! Are these those wonderful tears
That fashion and freshen for flight the terrible wings
    of the years ?
They fall on his smooth grey limbs as leaves that
    fall to the sea.
My vision is fevered, alas! for no Life is in tears nor
    in thee!
Thou art one of those golden mists that gladden the
    eyelids of youth
When Hope is the guiding-star ; and Love is the
    haven forsooth !
Avaunt thou powerless shape! To thy dreamland
    hence depart :
I alone will live at his lips and drink the dead tears
    at his heart.
And if my passionate plaint is not heard of the
    Gods on high,
I too will woo cruel death, and lie there beside
    him, and die.

IN CAMERA MORTIS.

POOR child ; when last I knew thy face,
Chidelessly fair and full of grace,—
Thy cheeks were glad with the light bright blood,—
Two very roses of womanhood,
Red-ripe with the springtide sun,
Lowly waiting to be won.
No rent lost lilies tangled wild
Amid these tresses ; but there smiled
As from the lips of some clear stream,
Or like thoughts of love in a virgin's dream,—
A garland of kingcups, golden as truth,
And thy vague blue eye seemed a vision of youth.
Oh child, poor child, and the waves of thine hair,
Like light fresh leaves of the springtime, fair,
Fell softly away in their shimmering ease,
As when a sweet forest-wind trembles the trees ;
And thy dead, wet hands were like flowerets gay,
Delighting in life, though life last but a day !
O moveless maiden ! what sorrow hath laden

Thy soul that our love could not shame it away ?
In the dark lone gloom of this little room,
Where the sun still woos the woodbine-bloom,
I watch for an hour, though the sunbeam-shower
Will never thy white lips illume.

II.

The wayward world on me too has hurled
Hard hail and the thunder of rage ;—
But I break not under the storms of its thunder!
And couldst thou not wait ?   Was it God or Fate,
That thy youth felt the anguish of age ?
There is no scorn upon thy lips ;
There is no anger in thine eyes :
But one sweet smile which doth eclipse
Death's agonies.
Thy bosom burns not,—speaks not now :—
And in the rhetoric of thy brow,
LOST LOVE alone replies.

DAWN ON CAPRI AND ISCHIA.

YCLAD in silver raiment, o'er the deep
   Capri looks forth toward her sister isle ;
   And Ischia greets her with the gentle smile
Of one awoke in wonder from sweet sleep.
Then they twain woo the Sun with yellow sheaves
   And glimmering fruit that costs no hand to dig,
   Moon-drooping lemons and the plastic fig ;
And little olives with undying leaves.
And all their skirts are tender with each hue
   That radiant maiden Iris ever wore ;
   Sea-flowers are there and scarlet madrepore :
And girdling these, the sea's unrivalled blue.

Dec. 29, 1879.

G

CONTENT.

No sound save awakening joy,
From the heart of maiden or boy
Is here when dawn sets crown
On the whispering olive-tree ;
And no forehead darkens to frown
When night falls sweetly down
  On the lids of the sea.

SORRENTO, *Jan.* 10, 1880.

THE LADY AND HER JUDAS-TREE.

I.

I WILL bury my grief in the garden,
  And put there a Judas-tree:
Bright flowers shall smile on its branches—
  A joy for the world and for me.
All day shall the birds be singing
  Blithe notes to the summer sun,
And take no thought for the grieving
  Of One whom Love hath undone.

II.

But at night when the breeze falls faintly
  Abroad from the fading west,
And the sweet birds heave in the shimmer
  Of moonlight that lulls them to rest;
O then will I go to my garden,
  I'll kneel by my Judas-tree,
And I'll pray high Heaven to pardon
  My Sweet for the sin done to me.

IN THE CASCINE, PISA, DEC., 1879.

LIKE a Cathedral,
Around us the forest,
Dreamy with vistas :
Dim in its vastness :—
Rooted in Silence !

Cloudy-veined columns
Blend into arches
Of blackening verdure,
Whose lessening myriads
Pillow the dove-white
Storms that are weary.

And on the undulant
Needle-strewn pavement
For sacred feet famous,
For passionate Shelley—
Apollo-like Byron,—
Veer the wild-violets
Kissed by the Zephyr.

Through the aisles gleaming,
Silver and golden
Spread there for ever
The dateless lichens
And fern-loving mosses ;
While in the transepts,
Little birds, chaunting,
Wander like pilgrims,
Loved by the spirit,—
Made bright for His worship.
Who gave them their voices.

And far, through the juniper,
Bashfully hiding,
Peeps the wild fallow ;—
Timidly listening
To the sweet trembling
Strings of the billows
Struck by the fingers
Of unseen spirits :—
Wafting our soul's-wings
Out o'er the twilight
Mediterranean!

IN DECEMBER.—"HEARTSEASE."

I.

IF I could but live till Spring!
    Ah! well-a-day!
Once more hear the sweet birds sing!
    Well-a-day!
I would watch the cradled flowers
Charm to smiles the April hours!
    Ah! well-a-day!

II.

But short and restless is the way;
    Ah! well-a-day!
Yet I see a brighter ray,
    Well-a-day!
Yet how would I, sweet Love, rejoice
To catch once more thy near, dear voice!
    Ah! well-a-day!

III.

I am pale and weary now ;

    Ah ! well-a-day !

His lips would cool my fevered brow ;

    Well-a-day ! well-a-day !

Could his strong arms but once more meet

Around my neck, ah ! 'twere too sweet !

His loved head on my shoulder lie !

With angel's bliss then mine would vie.

Yea, God,—one kiss before I die !

Is it too much ? Ah ! well-a-day !

MINIATURE.—VENICE.

ASLEEP are the voices ;
The sounds of the city ;
The city of waters !

Our gondola gliding
O'er the unrippled
Mystical highway,
Throbs the green oozes,
Sings to them, passing.

Lurid with lowering
Strokes of the sunset,
Beside us are leaning
The walls of the convent.

Above us the azure
Is trellised with tendrils
Of tempest-strewn cirrus.
What a sweet spirit
Of love is now blowing !

Close, to the southward,
Crownèd with poplar,
Lightens the Lido
In lone, sad splendour.
Night is behind it.

TO EMILIA S.

I.

THE buds are awakening ;
The small white petals,
Parted with sunlight,
Break into smiling.

II.

Out of the Winter,
The terror-born tempest,
They have arisen.
Yea, from the darkness,
Out of Death's empire ;
From under his throne
Of cold white ivory,
Broken to blossom,
They lean out sunwards.

III.

So, too, my darling,
Like the sweet April,

Grew the bright fingers
And beautiful eyelids
That lie in the dream-land
There on thy bosom.—
O for the gladness
That flowers from sorrow!

IV.

What kind great mother
Broke the dread sceptre
Held fearfully o'er thee?
Who baffled the despot?
Who spoiled him of glory?

V.

Thy windows are gleaming.
The mild sweet breezes
Stream o'er the crocus
And vale-born lilies,
On to thy beauties;
O friend, O beloved!
My greetings are with them.

THE EARL'S STORY.

ALL day my sense was dazzled with the dream :
   I wandered deftly through the autumn glens :
   And eveningwards her gentle handmaidens
Came by me singing like a silver stream.
Then She came softly, like the clear bright beam
   Of the new moon that glimmers through the fens ;
   And raimented like those fair citizens
Who make the might of Heaven so supreme.
And I that wooed her as a poor brown monk,
   At the high silver castle of her sire :—
   Whose heart was as a golden broken lyre ;
Whose body like an autumn-leaf had shrunk ;
There stood I all on fire at seeing her,
   And shining in my armour silverly,
   Behind the glory of an ancient tree
Whose branches cooled my cheeks with their sweet
     stir.
The little leaves and ferns that grew thereon

Seemed very parts of my emblazonry ;
So well dissembling to the passing eye
The splendid purpose that my soul had on.
And there she stopped ; though they went far along
And vanished like lost stars adown the wood :
Then seeing 'twas the spot where meet we should,
Like some lone bird she piped a little song.
Then, as a wispy flame, I leapt to her,
Gave her one kiss that hazard made not hard,
Strained to my breast the Lady Ermingard,
And led her swiftly to my Debonair.
Her willing feet like little glow-worms shone,
Hastening between the last November leaves ;
And like lit frost were her swallow-wingèd sleeves ;
And brighter still the light her eyes had on.
We rode all night, until we saw the sea ;
And my good squires and sailors in the barge,
Full well all gentlesse to us did discharge,
And urged the heavy craft right merrily.
And ere our eyes another night had seen,
Our holy friar gave her to be my wife.
Far more she loves me ; and most fair is life
While in my hall she sits,—my crownèd queen.

TOWARDS WINTER.

I.

NIGHT narrows in the shores of Day.
　And lo! the old, keen-fingered thief
Stealeth the seasons' rich array;
And the moon is a mist of gold and gray,
　Like a marigold broken and bowed with grief,
　Or an autumn-leaf.

II.

The sky above that spot was blue,
　Where now the Fates of Winter spin;
Love, there, lacked not its brightest hue,
And bright were the birds that therein flew,
　And sweet were the flowers, though tall and thin,
　That bloomed therein!

III.

Yet I'll believe that nothing dies.
　The poorest weed there lying prone

In blissful smiles will re-arise :
For all is pure in Love's fond eyes ;
   No evil thought in there hath flown :
   The Pure, alone !

IV.

And Love hath moved supremest there :
   For that garden kissed Love's golden face,
And the rosiest lips that ever were ;
And since it hailed Love's eyes and hair
   There came abroad in that sweet place,
   Perpetual grace.

SONG.

I AM going across the mountain,
   Where those sweet eyes cannot see me;
Where Beauty in one glorious fountain
   Fills the landscape bright and dreamy;
Which the sun is aye adorning
   With the jewels of his pride;
Where in rapture glows the morning
   Even as a joyful bride.
What will my old thoughts avail me
   When new thoughts usurp their reign?
New reflections will assail me!—
   Ah! but should We meet again!

SONNETS.

TO A LADY WHO BECAME A PREY TO MODERN PORTRAIT PAINTERS.

WHEN you by Angels to this Earth were brought
  With beauty brighter than the Heaven is blue ;
  Albeit, like all things rare, your days be few,
Upon your artist they cast never a thought !
How should they look on this your portrait, wrought
  By sheer grimace and blear-eyed interview,
  And give not pity-mingled smiles anew
O'er sad experience with presumption bought ?
There are less hues upon the flowers of May
  Than in your making Heaven did exercise :
And yet on you each Dauber must delay !
  What should a painter do ? or the art he plies ?
Lips hast thou like the farseen wings of Day :
  And Evening's earliest shadow 'neath your eyes.

H

THE ADORATION AT BETHLEHEM, BY GENTILE DA FABRIANO.

Reminiscences of three pictures at Florence.

I.

FROM Heaven unseen, a light as of the morn,
 The lowly Virgin with her child, reveals
 Before the pledge-spot where God brake the seals
Of Death, and Jesus Emmanuel was born.
Death is gone blind. His kingdom is forlorn.
 God now that blighting Tyranny repeals,
 And fashions from his Love a flower that heals
In hoary climes or scorching Capricorn.
And here doth wind full many a quaintly beast
 With spicy treasures of Arabia piled,
Whose owner rich-robed goes as to a feast;
 And sooty kings, from white South thrones beguiled;
And veteran emperors, from the glittering East,
 Bow down to serve their Saviour, though a child.

THE CORONATION OF THE VIRGIN, BY FRA FILIPPO.

2.

ON each side in the sunlit chancel stand

   Sweet silver companies of singing spring.

   Bright garlands round their brows are flowering:

Fresh lilies hover above each hidden hand:

And linking these fair choral streams, a band

   Of saintly men and women, priest and king—

   Kneeling, a festive symphony do sing,

With cherub-wingèd children of the land.

E'en as a star within the crescent moon,

   So, in this choir of most divine renown,

The mother of Christ entreats immortal boon;

   And over where she prayeth, kneeling down,

The stiff-coped hoary priest is bent; and soon

   On her meek head will set God's golden crown.

BOTTICELLI'S APHRODITE

3.

A WIDE-WINGED silver shell beneath her feet,
   The foam-born Goddess lonely wanders-on :
   Her dove-white body softly blown upon
By the linked Zephyrs' unreluctant sweet ;
And Spring's impassioned roses falling fleet,
   Strain but to touch their queen-companion :
   And from the whispering shore now well-nigh won,
Flora with redolent gift leans forth to greet ;
And all the little Cyprian waves are singing
   Round the poised labouring shell : and from the trees
That darken out the sun's desire, are ringing
   Virginal voices of birds that seek Love's ease
   Not unpropitiously from Her who sees
All sorrow : yet all joy is ever bringing.

AT DANTE'S TOMB.

As old Ravenna in her radiancy
  (As every line of her worn body tells)
  For fervent love and chequered life excels
All other daughters of sweet Italy ;—
So dost thou, DANTE, through the heart's blue sky,
  Outsoar thy kindred of the sacred well :
  Nor come I here to wake a funeral knell
For One made glad through all Eternity.
She was thy bride in Life : her bridegroom thou :
  Her deathless beauties were thy marriage-feast :
Her azure sky, a garland for thy brow :
  Her immemorial grove—thy splendid priest
That raised his hands : then at thy feet did bow,—
  As I do, here :—thy brother, last and least !

   Nov. 12, 1879.

A LANDSCAPE.

BRIGHT ridges broken of the riotous sun
   To voiceful vallies glad with living gold,
   And opiate flowers that in the days of old
Their blameless, deathless dynasty begun.
Around these airy islands, softly spun
   (E'en as a vision in dream), a vestal fold
   Of flushed, fond, clinging cloud : and o'er the wold,
The sharp, undreaded shadows wildly run.
And all the reasonless light air doth reel
   With a sweet restless song, poured from above :
(Like a bright promise of Joy, that makes us feel
   The fiery rainbow and the faithful dove
   Symbols of immortality and Love) :—
And, far beyond, a sun-swept water-wheel.

A VISION OF THREE THINGS BEAUTIFUL.

How swift Life's million-coloured stream runs by!
　We seem as trembling willows on its verge.
　Thousands of sorrows darkle 'neath a surge
That wins its glitter from a twilight sky.
But Light itself and Love like Angels fly
　Above the furious waters: and there merge
　Soft mysteries in Music's sweetest dirge :—
These three make up our dear Mortality.
O ye fair dove-eyed spirits of the stream,
　In whose close union is divine delight,—
　Yea, in whose dazzling beauty my poor sight,—
(Like a dull thought out-brightened in a dream
That outsoars bliss),—now fades as a fitful beam ;
　Which is the mightiest ? Music, or Love, or Light ?

TO E. C.

I.

LIFE'S night is dark.   Our open eyes are blind.
  In fearful trustfulness we creep along :
  Yet haply hear betimes the tender song
Of Love's sweet-bird or feel the flower-soft wind !
We wander from the paths that were designed.
  Our limbs are feeble though our souls are strong.
  We feel the right : but ever choose the wrong,
Although the goal is never hard to find.
Our souls should be our angels for to guide
  Our failing feet :—to make dark life bright day,—
And turn Queen Death to be our subject-bride.
  How dread then would it be for me to stray
From the true path, had I not at my side
  Thee, sweet companion, for Life's weary way !

II.

Time hath made interval betwixt us twain.

  This stream a brook was ere it grew a stream.

  Men must be humble would they be supreme!

Though all things die, and none may long remain!

Mine is the Youth: then mine the Great to gain.

  You see the actual, and I dream the dream,

    And Life, like a flame, flows soft 'twixt each extreme!

Between these two, what may we not attain?

Age, Manhood, Youth,—one Deity controuls :—

  Diversely led to innocence or crime.

Each, as he dies, is't not the same bell tolls?

  Youth, Manhood, Age, may all be made sublime.

Years are the subjects of all kingly souls ;

  Feeling,—the true Republic of all Time!

IN MEMORIAM . J. F. BOYES.

WHILES thou wert here upon this world of ours,
    I knew of nought that might with thee compare :
    For things most mean but touched thee, and were
        fair :
And the bare winter trees seemed filled with flowers.
Sweet labours fell from thee like April showers,
    Fresh'ning with kindly drops the scorched air :
    For where they fell they pelted out dull Care,
And turned poor cots forlorn to blissful bowers.

But now thou'rt gone ; my memory is on fire :
    Death is more subtle than sweet Song can tell,
That rings this music from my silent lyre.
    About thy cheerful dwelling breathed a spell
Which bade me e'en the dull brown bricks admire ;—
    And now one needs must love the tomb as well.

TO E. S.

I.

FIRST flower of Spring about my frozen soul,
    Leaning thy beauty on the unfost'ring air—
    (Where thy white scutcheon pleads than snow more
        fair)—
Can'st thou face hero-like thy later dole?
Dost thou not catch the Future's dismal tone
    Shading the Present: purpling things that Were?
    Or of To-come, dost thou make yet no care:—
Dealing with what is here, in strong Controul?
Lend me thy Love's keen sword to steel my
        thigh:—
    To cleave the dragons that around me hiss:—
To prove on hateful phantoms that flit by!
    For thy bright soul, being guide, nought can
        amiss:
Thy daintiest ringlet for to win or die,
    And for my guerdon thy sweet lip to kiss!

II.

Hail, Holy power! whose bliss-diffusing wing
   Dowers our want with that true opulence
   Which turns each chill doubt that assaults our
      sense
Into warm Faith,—as the sun turns frost in Spring!
Like the swart Indian wizard, thou dost bring
   Abounding beauty in glad confidence,—
   Flowers and leaves, and gentle redolence,
From merest mould: whereof Renown doth sing!
Loves humble home that I would eternize
   Nestles for meekness lower than the rest:
They are as like each other as dull flies.
   The streets are dull too: yet Love doth invest
That sweet abode with beauties manifest:
   And any street there leads to Paradise.

III.

Before me stood bright Beauty,—sweet unknown :—
   Syren, my soul desired: unseen before;
   Treasure my song delights in lingering o'er:
Feeling thereat I waste no days alone.
Over her blameless ears much gold was blown,

Like rhyming ripplets on a silver shore.
And ah! my Life, my Love, desired her more
For the still splendour that below them shone.
Her lips were music-shapen : wrought as well
  As is the lyre for song,—for kisses free
Felt sweetness drifted through their gentle swell.
  But her clear subtle neck's poised ivory
Seemed most of all her sovereign soul to tell,
  Who, silent then, is now most heard of me.

IV.

Some have compared their Love to a rare dream
  Whose magic lineaments through life remain,
  Painted in fadeless passion on the brain ;
Whose mere remembrance makes a life supreme.
And, natheless, Love in its most sweet extreme,
  Makes Poets of us all.   While Love's warm rain
  Washes our bodies, we are free from stain.
Therefore are poets held in strange esteem.
Some, through their Love, see bliss in every flower ;
  Some fit Love's song to every bird that sings :
Their passion fluctuates each plastic hour.
  But I can bear no web about my wings ;

Since I loved you, no sole sweet thing has power :
  I prey on all the Beauty of all things.

V.

Rough rocks are solely rough, to wilful eyes.
  The sea—a puking-place to wormy souls :
  Each has a law of being that controuls
The bane or beauty of what things arise.
Some, rueful chimes in sweet notes recognize :—
  Dread shelving deeps where others figure shoals :
  Others see mountains in the stir of moles :—
Life everlasting in each thing that dies.
Natheless, dark things are done beneath the sun ;
  Yet seld is seen an utter starless night.
  All things I wis do poise their discords right :
But if true harmony on Earth be none ;
  We will at least tune Life, in Hate's despite,
And pitch our Loves in perfect unison.

VI.

Now being parted from you for a space
  (Though cursing Fortune for her fell escheats),
  I revel in your recollected sweets,

And banquet sleep with dreams of your embrace.
Though other Poets do delight to trace
   The prickly battle-field of their defeats :
   Their vain advances and their raged retreats :—
I only laud Good-Fortune and your face.
Sometimes, set jewel-wise in your dear room
   I see your eye,—like that wee plunderer,
The furred bee,—feasting on some liege volùme.
   At other times I see you soft, astir
Where those blest constellated lilies bloom :
   Yourself, like some tall morning Sunflowèr.

VII.

Sometimes, when lonely and afar from her
   Who is the daylight to my darkened soul,—
   My patient mind by Time's quick stream doth troll
Casting for Beauty long ensconcèd there.
Far down lie shapely treasures without stir :
   Splendour bespoilèd 'neath his rude controul.
   Is that our great Hope's end ?—our hapless goal ?
Is that the blessing Heaven will feign confer ?
Then doubtful mourn I, sweets for me unmeant :
   For dear enjoyments that cannot accrue :

And Beauty seeming through past Time mis-
    spent,
    Solely one truth Life's rapture doth renew
That Past and Present in one sure concent
    Mete forth their five-fold melodies in You.

VIII.

When from my friendly books at length I part ;
    And a refreshment rare, I would beget,
    Childlike I creep to my blest cabinet,
And thence unhasp the volume of your heart.
As in some lordly hall the walls athwart,—
    Each gentle portrait, crest and banneret ;—
    So in your Hallowed leaves are sweetly set
Love's scutcheons limned with most alluring art.
When some great mortal hies to Death's abode ;—
    Then, for grave pleasure, Men tire not con-
        triving
To praise and picture forth the path he trode.
    Then, how supreme a gift is Fortune giving ;—
Making me lord of your Life's episode ;
    Who, at the same time grants you to me,
        living !

IX.

Till I loved You, I reasoned like the rest—
    That happiness was not for Humankind :—
    Friendship but transient ; and true Love, confined :
Howe'er we may devise to make us blest !
But You, sweet Love, are such an alchemist
    That from stored Sapience, you have now
      combined
    To mould the dull dross of my ravelled mind,
And gloss it so to grave you manifest.
Thus Fancy oft makes reason of things mad !
    Hears in quaint discords, subtle harmony :—
And joyful echoes under sounds most sad.
    But since my change, so sweet content am I :
I love thee more for all my Love hath had ;—
    And of new joys have no necessity.

X.

Why don't you come to us, my sweet E——ie ?
    Come and divine this soft Atlantic air :
    Come and join hands with us; our wand'ring share
Where clustering wild-flowers company the sea !
What mean enticements for your sympathy

I

Those forcèd sweets that prove the season bare,—
   Those quack-marred features, and that midnight
      glare !
Come, like a wild-flower ; like a wave, be free.
'Tis true we have no balls, no plays, no dinners ;—
   Not even parties worth a dainty glove :
Yet did all Mayfair cast, we might be winners ;
   And I will whisper to my little dove
How we're so good, that we would fain be sinners,—
   Were there not One alone who sways our Love.

XI.

Yes ! being quit that prone Cyclopean net,
   Whose every mesh is true joy's mockery ;—
   One sole sweet image can my soul descry,
As on an evening when one star is met :—
Or as Madonna limned by Tintoret :
   Where all the air of Heaven's divinity
   Is grained with golden smiles : yet her blue eye
Beams with a love no gazer can forget :—
Or as a sunbeam slanted from above,
   Through sullen clouds of languid August day ;

Where Fancy's hand would poise the sacred
    dove :—
Or as the heart when all its huge array
  Of Passion makes life's gloom a holiday
And glows with one out-bright'ning flame of Love.

XII.

Whether I dream in bowers of bright recess ;—
  Or lose myself in Music's softest art ;
  Or flee on Fancy's wings, to some sweet part
Where dwell the dreams of Poets :—I confess,
From You, each hour doth borrow loveliness,
  Catching enduring colours from your heart,
  Which, as a fount, is, whence doth blithely start
Fresh Life that silvers out my past distress.
Then, Beauty, mine,—you'll not ungentle be
  If the return, though it comes springing true,
Seems but in sooth, a feeble gift, to Thee.—
  Of such surpassing sweet—so ever new
Is this bright Love you lavish so on me ;—
  It were not possible from me to You.

XIII.

Vainly I railed at Man's inconstancies;
  And in his various features tried to trace
  Each several evil lurking 'neath each grace.
This was the end of my philosophies.
Love only, fixeth all Man's qualities,
  That through the storms of health and age and place
  Roots the heart firmer; and upon the face
Transforms all evils to their contraries!
In Life's dark sea, though faced to frequent shock,
His soul as a beacon on some frowning rock,
  Love's humanizing light doth soft distil;
And when Death in his kindly arms doth lock
  The world that woos him,—be 't for good or ill,—
  Man's soul upon its high-place burneth still!

THE TWO SEASONS OF THE POET.

THIS is the season when Love's nights grow cold :
    It is the gold vale to the travelling year,
    Where rosy maids do chide the gossamer,
And all the woodland whispers, dripping gold.
And here is the other season, when the wold
    A lake of emerald glory doth appear ;
    And evenings, rose-like, widen for to hear
The joyous passion that all things unfold.
Yet, though they yield the leaves that shape his crown,
They are but sands, where the Poet's high renown
    Is built, so subject to the waves profane.
    They make too Life's hourglass that so flows
        amain :—
Autumn comes here ;—the leaves are falling down :—
    And when Spring comes, the leaves are there again!

RHODIAN SWALLOW-SONG.

SEE, we greet thee beautiful, night-plumed angel,
Southward o'er our Mediterranean azure :—
Dallying round our guardian-altars,—Darkly-
　　　　Delicate Swallow!
Lo! thou cowerest, worried of wing and silent!
Did the rude north whirlwind revere thy dwelling?
Or did snake-like billows devour thy children,—
　　　　Pilot of Beauty?
Or hast thou felt some phantom-swift, scythe-billed
　　　tyrant,
Fiend-like haunting, that thou art tired and throbbing,
Grieved though in safety,—noteless of sweet new
　　　courtship,—
　　　　Friended of all men?
Welcome, loved one! Here will the soft air feast
　　　thee.
Flee thy heart's-cloud.　Marble-rimmed pools for
　　　coursing

Here thou'lt find, and citron-lit capes for soaring,
      Cooling at noontide.
Here thy nest, on glittering, songful temples,
May'st thou surely fasten in freedom, guest-wise;
Blessed from tempest; held from profane, fleet falcons,
      Exquisite swallow!

MUSIC AND THE POET.

MUSIC is the Poet's friend,
Who with Life and Light doth blend.
She wafteth him up on her eagle wings
 Into the morning heaven :
Where he sees immortal things—
 Whence his gifts are given.
Him loves She by night and day :
 Grieves with him in his strife :
 And when he gives up Life,
Love-like, she beareth him far away.

KILGRIMAL: A LEGEND.

I.

WHILOM an ivied church did smile

From Kilgrimal's cloistered isle;

Where the infant billows leaping,

Seemed their wild-flower pleasance reaping.

Each one, rapt by the toying breeze

Silver'd o'er the cypress-trees

(That like sentinels dark and dread

Guarded well the dateless dead);

And pied with foam the smiling flowers

That turned dull graves to blithesome bowers.

And O for that merry peal of bells

That broke across to the mainland dells;

Bidding all who heard it sing

" Peace, like to-day's, to-morrow bring !"

Many death did bravely meet,

Seeing their sepulchre so sweet.

II.

But now the angry rollers roar
Where Kilgrimal smiles no more :
Cypress-trees and all are fled
To the kingdom of the dead.
Save, as folk tell how sailing there
Quivers at heart each mariner,
While a dismal, jaunting chime,
Hoarsely fetched and out of time,
Breaking from the depths below,
Sways the phantoms as they go,
Risen from their ancient sleep
To vex the watchers of the deep.
For all things fair that sweetly smiled,
In the quick-sand deeply piled ;—
Massed in one triumphant grave—
The young, the beautiful, the brave,—
Lie, like lumps of potter's clay,
Waiting till the shaping-day
When erst the glorious beam of light
Shall pierce the horror of their night ;
Heaven's own with mercy to befriend,
Eke make of loathen things an end.

III.

Then shall that island of the west
Peer, like a sweet bird from her nest,
Where the rose-lipped zephyrs driven
Breathe o'er all the sea of Heaven.

BOLOGNA, *Nov.* 7, 1879.

PARAPHRASE FROM THE ARABIC OF ABDALRAHMAN.

" BEAUTIFUL Palm-tree,
Thou too, art an exile ;—
Airs of Algarbe
Court thee and kiss thee :
While towards Heaven,
Thy head is uplifted
In stately splendour !

"Ah ! but how bitter
The moan of thy branches,
Could'st thou look backward :—
Our cradle remembering !
Alone I am tasting
The wine of affliction
That withers my inmost ;—
My youth and my glory.

"Once I was weeping
Beside thy sisters :
Soothing Love's sorrow

By Forat's sweet waters,
That wander so softly !

" But they, and their river,
And Thou, my dear country,
No memory ownest
Of me or my sorrow !
Yet for Thee shall I never
Stay my lamenting,
Or close up the flowing
Eyelids of anguish.
Thus, I uplift me
To the same starlight,
And falling down earthward
On alien flowers,
Break into mourning,
Till I am no longer
To Earth or to Heaven,
Known or belonging."

THE TRANCE OF WINTER.

GONE to his fathers,—
His grey dead parents,
Fretful, lamenting
Withering Winter!
His murky stiff garments
Are gathered together,
Carelessly hiding
His shrunken white limbs.
No wreaths of new flowers:—
No virginal blossoms
Brighten with smiling
The sad soft twilight,
Where he is lying!
Only a chorus
Of virginal voices
Weaves through his casement—
(His broken north window)—
Beautiful visions.
Things He has felt not,

Being cold-hearted,

Yet are vibrating

Through his pale body ;

Faintly are thrilling

Through the unfeeling

Limbs of the soul-less !

Children can see not

The signs of his living.

He breathes not : he speaks not !

Yet to the aged

Eyes of experience,

Though closen his eyelids,

He is but sleeping ;

Wasted with labour.

He will be waking :—

Laying his finger

Icily on them ;

Who shall dare vex him ?

April 25, 1880.

VINTAGE-SONG.

UNDER this peerless southern sky,
　　Amid a bower of fiery leaves
And eddying tendrils, we do ply
　　Our hands to pluck the purple sheaves.
　　　　And, down the mountain-height,
　　　　The torrent, dashing bright,
　　A woof of silver music ever weaves.
It weaves the song of the rose-crowned years
That steals the hearts of the vintagers.
　　　　It sparkles along
　　　　In its streaming song
Like wine that aye the spirit-fallen cheers.
　　Chorus: It sparkles, &c.

BAVENO, *Oct.* 14, 1879.

LIFE.

I.

MAN'S life is as a sea-girt rock.
Over him with foam and shock
   Wild sorrows are breaking :
      Trouble and sin
      Girdle him in,
   His beauty for ever taking.

II.

Over his glittering shoulders rush
With alternate roar and hush,
   The hurtling billows.
      Like morn aglow
      His glorious brow :
   His feet in the soft sea-pillows.

K

III.

Hour by hour, and day by day,

He is wearing fast away ;

Made deaf by the rattle.

Time and the sea

No mercy decree

Till he break in the teeth of the battle.

JANE SHORE.

" Is Peace too gone from thy ways with the face of thy
  guardian King ?—
O Beauty of all men's praise !   O broken and profit-
  less thing !
Must Thou bow down to the feet of them thou hast
  feasted and clothed ?
Must thou learn from lips that were sweet, how now
  thou art flouted and loathed ?
I stand as an Angel above thee ; my pinions are bright
  on the blast :
Dost deem there is one that still loves thee ; or Love
  that will save thee at last ?

" I see the strange stir of the city ; they gather from
  every part
To be gay at thy shame.   Is Pity gone blind in the
  maze of Man's heart ?—

Their murmur, like dull drawn thunder, invades the
    moist ways of the air ;
Thy fair face smites them asunder ! Jane Shore, why
    art thou so fair ?

" I see them grown dumb and afraid in their gait, as
    thou goest along ;
And curse-stricken things to be said, turn soft on each
    eraven tongue !

'O Blind and Piteous nation, this hour art thou tor-
    tured and driven !
This day is thy dark lamentation gone up as a blight
    into heaven.
Thou art fettered and crushed as in prison :—a sore in
    the whole world's sight.
Ah ! when shall we see thee arisen, and arrayed in
    the beauty of light ?
Thou art smitten with tyrannous hands: thou art
    harassed with cankering chains.
Will the eyes of the beaten lands compassion the sight
    of thy pains ?

" Even she,—this fair mute daughter of men, was the
    pride of thy King !

Behold how thy King hath wrought her a wound from
    the keen world's sting !

His purple is set on her shoulders—Her step is the gait
    of a queen :

Brightening her gloomy beholders with beauty in
    gliding between.

Calm in heavenly assurance, her sins are made clean
    in God's sight :

Meek with heroic endurance, like a lone star set in the
    night !—

No Beauty becometh the wearer so chideless as her's
    this day :

Than her heart, is anything fairer ?—Is it April or
    May ?

There is nothing : no star in Heaven beams down with
    a brighter ray

Though the storm-clouds of Sorrow are driven to
    darken her wintry way.

" O woman, far-fallen ! most-tempted ! a pledge thou
    art come to redeem !

And though vials of sin thou hadst emptied ; repen-
    tance had made thee supreme.

A crown of light, with my fingers, I fix on thy lumi-
    nous brow :

In my ear the Lord's jubilant angels re-anthem delight
    in thee now."

"And thou, hard husband of Earth! behold the
    bright girl of thy prime !

Dost remember her leaving thy hearth for the hearth
    of her King on a time ?

Oh think how thy lips have kissed her—thy blood hath
    mixed with her life.

Is thy soul not vext with a blister ?—Was this angel
    of women thy wife ?—

Didst thou burn thy heart in her beauty, and breathe
    the sweet feeling of Peace ?

And now, must thy damnable duty attaint and annul
    Love's Lease ?

Hast thou once felt the shape of her face ?—Hast loved
    her a night and a morn,

And canst see now her womanly grace so held to the
    arrows of scorn ?

"Oh Man, in the reason of things, this renders the
 noontide so black!

And bringeth my shadowing wings abroad in thy
 desolate track!

Her sin was the sin of thy fashion as it for ever hath
 been ;—

But natheless the want of compassion ;—God deems
 this the deepest sin!"

A MORAL COLLOQUY.[1]

CRICKET.

Now little Death-watch tell me what
  Gave birth to this strange notion
That maids at hearing you, turn hot
  And cold in dire emotion!
Merely to hear thy tiny tick
Tells as sure as the candle-wick
  Mischief to their devotion!

DEATH-WATCH.

I too will ask Sir Cricket why
  While yet he me importunes,
That catching his peculiar cry
  Maids augur their good fortunes?

CRICKET.

Ah! that your mere good sense might tell you,
  Little cupboard elf,
Since my tune will aye compel you
  Of its own sweet self;

[1] *Vide* " English Folklore," page 135.   T. F. Dyer.

And sweet things find a sheltering snood
In the fair breast of maidenhood !

DEATH-WATCH.

Poor mankind !   How sad and foolish
   Are your fancyings !
You own gifts but make you mulish
   In less worthy things.
From my hole within this wicket
   Clearly can I see
How infected is the cricket
   With your vanity.

I would rather not awaken
   Praise for me nor blame :
But continue, though mistaken,
   Honestly the same.

PARIS.

I.

BEAUTIFUL City!
Peerless Paris!
Splendid in Majesty
Over all cities!
Joy-giving plenty
Glows through the smiling
Lips of thy children:
And in their mansions
Shine the sweet triumphs
Of artist and soldier,
Gathered together
For sovereign dominion:
Thee as their guardian,—
Their beautiful mistress,—
Terrible Paris!

II.

Yet through thy splendour
My vain eyes are searching
For heirlings of Beauty
That teem, like the affluent
Olive, in England ;
Who smile on the pilgrim
Wafting his spirit
Into Elysium :—
Native and artless
As the enchantment
Of a wild wood-note :—
Stamping a marvel
Into firm manhood.
All thy rich glitter
Seen in entirety,
Heaped in Divinity,
Is not so holy
As that which I find not.

BOADICEA AND THE HARE.

STANDING amid her burning squadrons,
　　Boadicea made a sign :
　　Straight arose a shrill wild whine,
As an hare broke from her bosom
　　That the augurs might divine.

" What," say all, " will be your finding :—
　　You, wise men, who know the stars ?"
　　" Look how she will cover regions,
With her twisting and her winding."
　　Then the lightning-heart of legions
　　Tore the air with wild huzzas.
And the clanking chariot-rattle
　　Drove them on their deadly way :
Britain's Lady led the battle :
　　And we know who won the day.

THEN AND NOW.

WHEN last I faced thy smile, mute friend, of social
    charms I knew no need :—
Lingering through the merry mead ·where summer
    kissed each finger's end.
Little crowns we wove of wild white rose, and a
    wreath for your Wife's bright hair.
And never I learned—(as she well knows)—the grey-
    rose gathering there.
But now in dreams a dismal knell bids me o'er Acheron
    be gone,
Where in meads of mournful Asphodel, I glean the
    like her head has on !

SUMMER-STORM.

ASLEEP are the branches!
Not one lone murmur
Comes from the tree-tops
Through the dread darkness!
Stars of the summer,
Southward to northward,
Are quenched by the grisly-
Garmented Thunder:
And fast through the blackness
The flail of the lightning
Is smiting the prone, long
Indolent rain-clouds:
Which the stilled river
Playfully mimics
Over the meadows.
While from the flower-sweet

Lips of the mid-night
Grumbles the distant
Muttering thunder,—
Grimly impatient.

SHIPLAKE HOUSE, *Aug.,* 1880.

BEFORE THE TUILERIES, 1880.

I.

WHERE hath the glory of Empire fled :—
The lightnings of its lifted head ?
 Where is the strength its arms had on :—
The sword of gold that burned and bled ?—
  The fame that in the Father shone,
   And in the Son ?

II.

Before me stand their palace-walls ;
Fire last hath feasted in the halls,
 And smoke hath plied its baleful wings.
The roof-let rain on no one falls,
 Save on dim ghosts of bygone things,
  Whose silence stings.

III.

And rabbling, sham Republic rears
Its snaky locks through blood and tears,
 And dares to dream of staying France.

But when at last she eager, hears
 Empire arise : with fire and lance
  She shall advance !

IV.

And in its own confounded toils,
The horrors of its blood-stained coils,
 This monster shall be slain outright.
Its head,—too foul for victor's spoils,—
 Shall be cast out beyond our sight
  To utter night.

V.

Then on her bright, long-hidden throne,
Beauty and Queen, in glory grown,
 She shall the fadeless land defend.
The German eagles shall be prone :
 And Albion at her side,—her friend
  Unto the end !

L

SONG.

I.

I WAS a little birdlet fair,—
   The nurseling of the breeze.
I sang upon Life's golden air
   Amid the woodland trees.

II.

O I was so glad in the spring-tide soft :
   Though grief my heart now wrings !
And I cry to the breezes to lift me aloft :
   But Love hath broken my wings.

THE LAST LION OF GRENADA.[1]

PART I.

I.

By an iron battle-tide,
Sore beset on every side,
Smiled, though broken to the core,
The Queenliest city of the Moor!
Shattered shone Grenada's walls:—
Burnt,—unroofed, her princely halls;
And Famine whined from door to door.

II.

All her lean-faced turbaned sages,
Met in council skimmed the pages
   Of the terms of Ferdinand.
There, with mighty lamentation,
All the last hope of the nation

[1] *Vide* Washington Irving, ch. xcvi.

Tottering seemed to stand :—
" If ye yield to these conditions,
I will fill ye with provisions ;
 And again shall smile your land."

III.

The prospect of abandoned fears
Dimmed their glassy eyes with tears :—
 Filled some hearts with gratitude.
Only on one among them all,
Idly seemed those words to fall,
 And alone, apart, he stood.

IV.

" Craven drops should but illumine
Cheeks of hungry helpless women.
 A man's tears should be tears of blood !
If our kingdom must surrender,
Death is still our best defender !—
 Death will be our glory-hood."

V.

When he ceased, there was no sound:
And his King looked wildly round.
But upon their care-worn faces
Not one lordly change he traces.
    Honour!—what care starved men of it?
A moment still Boabdil sate;
Then, rising, spake he: "God is great!
    And Mahomet is his prophet!"
"As to Fate, however come it,
Fate He sways,—our Lord Mahomet!"
    "And to Earth's none other hark we!"
    Echoed Vizier and Alfaqui.
Ah! it was a fearful thing
To see them press so round their King!

VI.

But Muza,—in a furnace-heat, he
Saw them crush to sign the treaty:
So he cried:—" Before this eve
The faithless Spaniard will deceive.
Of all the evils threat'ning here,
Death is the last a Moor should fear:—

For your sensual harmless maggot,
Out beyond there, flames the faggot:
And for the daggers ye should plunge on !—
Is Death more dire than fetid Dungeon ?
Though these terms seem Life's gold hem,
I will never stoop to them."

VII.

Leaving thus those craven sages
To the hate of after-ages,
And their yet-surviving scions ;—
Then, across the court of Lions
Strode he, torn with silent Pity.
  Death to him was no alarmer :—
  So he donned his cloudy armour,
And at twilight left the city.

PART II.

I.

IT is the night!   With passion, eager
Rides he where amid the Vega
   Xenil winds her waters fair.
Fourteen Andalusian lances
Spy the Moor in the river's glances,
   And they bid him: "Stand! Declare!"

II.

Where he cleaves, the air is singing;
And his courser's hoofs are ringing
   As they smite the stones to fire.
Than a giant seems he larger
On his lightning-footed charger,—
   In his terrible attire.

III.

Like a lion that Anger wings,
Into their midst this champion springs,
   And spins their leader to the ground.

And he smites and slays remorseless
Till a javelin leaves him horseless ;
   And his foes rage all around !

IV.

Like a demon armed with flames,
Still he slays where'er he aims,
   Brandishing his scimitar.
Wounded sore, at last he shouts
" Allah Achbar !" while he flouts
   From the ground the unequal war.

V.

And when he could no longer battle :—
" Slay me not as ye slay cattle,"
   Cried he, " with your farrier's fleam ;
Never will Muza brook coercion !"—
And with one last—one wild exertion—
   Hurled himself into the stream.

A SEA-PEARL.

I.

I WENT out in the gloaming,
   Along the lone sea-shore:
And I felt like a wanderer roaming
   O'er some bleak cloudy moor.

II.

Despair, like a clammy snake,
   Around my heart did curl:
When the sun, as it were for my sake,
   Shone down at my feet on a pearl!

III.

I brought it afar from the billow,
   And gave it my Heart for a guest:
I laid it, for luck, by my pillow:
   But I found it more loved my breast

IV.

But the billows now call me cruel :

   And sing 'twixt a frown and a smile :—

"O give to us back our jewel!

   What hast thou been doing the while?"

I.

'ONCE, O Earth, thy presence chilled me
　With its man-inflicted scars :
Mystic dreams and visions filled me,
　And my heart lived with the stars.

II.

But since thy spirit flashed across me,
　I can neither dream nor rest :
And from my frigid stars, I toss me,
　Warm, delirious, to thy breast !

MAN.

QUICK to see and quicker to feel :
   Man ever delights in extremes.
One moment he clings to the real :
   The next he is rapt in his dreams !

STANZAS. AT VENICE.

I.

THY water-ways are silent now :
　The eventide is sweet and clear :
The full moon, cloven by our prow,
　Gleams faintly on the gondolier.
Noiseless as night, we glide between
　The oozy fields of trembling green ;—
(Save the wild whisperings of the stream
That make the dimness round us seem
　Like Life's own dream.)

II.

The Lido lightens in the breath
　That beams against the tide ;
Her misty leaves look up like Death—
　Life's pale, cold underside.
I view the flood's uncertain peace ;
I watch the war amid the skies ;
But, far above, I see release

In calm that never dies.
Love! let me press thy soul to me:
That we together one may be,
Immortally!

III.

Thy day, too, strews its dying flowers,
　　Like these along the failing west;
And twilight in the changing hours
　　Bears them on her placid breast.
Oh might thy glories in this hour
Arise, my Venice, in full flower;
I would not pray,—I would not lift
To thy sweet lips a kiss for gift;
But I would cleave to thee for aye;—
Until death's own Imperial sway
Closed out my day!

IV.

Yea! Love's own breath is blowing here;
　　Love's lips and fingers mix together,
Even as these leaves and ripples, dear,
　　Mix in the Autumn weather.

Out of the ashes of our sorrow
Rises merriment to-morrow.
Twilight loves the softest tunes
Luted among her lone Lagunes.
Venice may have lived her day,
Lion-wise is she at bay:
But true Love knoweth no decay.
Well-a-day!

SONG.

I.

THROUGH Dunster's sombre paths divine
I chanced to wander, Love, this morning.
Full many a thought of thee and thine,
  Their yew-shade deep, My Sweet, adorning.

II.

A wanton storm had strewn the ways,
  Like that which spoiled the Spanish galleons ;
Branches and buds and fragrant sprays
  Lay fading by in torn battalions.

III.

Methought, as I was passing there,
  Fate's merciless hand was heavy on them.
" How sweet !" they seemed to say, " Death were"
  (Could your fond eyes but smile upon them).

IV.

Then as I gazed down on the park,
   Gay fallow-deer were footing featly ;
And high in Heaven the hidden lark
   Was uttering things that moved me sweetly.

DUNSTER, *Aug.* 10, 1880.

VERSES ON AN OLD CHURCH.

I.

STILL dost thou chime the hours that pass thee by,—
　　Thou dim grey church, whose towers
Point o'er the hill-side on the pale-green sky,
　　Mocking dull time that devours.

II.

The trees that fair hands planted at thy birth
　　Stretch haggard on the air :
Life scarcely seems to bind them to the Earth,—
　　Dark emblems of despair.

III.

They watched the centuries that snowed thine head,
　　The sunshine and the murk ;—
Thought it thine end when the Usurper's tread
　　Made waste thy carven-work.

IV.

But thou each century dost safely brave,
   (Though they shall brave no more);
Even as the swimmer faceth a full wave,
   Though it waft him to the shore.

V.

Chime on thy chimes, thou church so dim and grey,
   Fear not the Traitor Time!
So beautiful thy ancient strength to-day;
   Thy ruin were sublime.

   MINEHEAD.

LUCA SIGNORELLI.

" Let no man name death to me ! It is a word infinitely
terrible."—Vitt. Corrombona. J. Webster.

I.

Come, civil Twilight, rosy-mantled maid,
 With thy rare damask flush this deathful room
Where the lost glory of my Life is laid,
 Even as a sweet dead day in Time's dull tomb.
 Yea ! ere his soft eyes shrink in lasting doom,
Let thy bright fingers soothe his sleeping brow
 And to my vision his pale lips illume.—
Pity, sweet Goddess, while I here avow
That I have loved Day's beauty more than thine,—
  till now !

II.

All giant-like, in silence sinks the sun.
 His crimson ministers about him cling,
Believing not his reign, so gay begun,

Can cease in Night—He seeming Nature's King!
Over the azure heaven he doth fling
The ribbons of his golden-claspèd snood,
    As though the venturous breezes would him bring
Fresh reinforcement for defeated Good ;—
But yon dark-banded mist o'erwhelms his gloryhood.

III.

So, too, have I shone with full-rounded Hope,
    Holding my swerveless course through Life's
        swect air ;
Finding in yon dead shape my soul's full scope
    For the expanded deity that's there.
    Ev'n as some poet on a mountain fair,
Scarce halting at its summit, from each part
    Of girdling Nature, feeling splendours rare
Drink out his failing spirit,—with a start,
As in a dream, clasps all the beauty to his heart ;—

IV.

So did I feel while life glowed there in Him.
    I was held poor in what Man treasure deems.
I drained Life's alchemy down from the brim,

He being the cup; and even my sternest themes
    Were tempered by the magic that yet dreams
Around his losing lines ;—for I well saw
    That men desirèd most the clearest streams ;—
And from a deep, clear spring, by Man's own law,
Each thirster pays the well-man for the draw.

V.

His gifts were like the flowering isles that rise
    Through radiant morning, where the very mist
That melts and mantles round, to reverent eyes
    Seems veil for their divinity. O list !—
    'Twas but the evening wind that deftly kissed,
And blew a helden blossom from his hand,
    As if to shame the blast of Death that hissed,
Stinging my ears, along Life's blooming strand ;—
That made belovèd paths mere wilderness of sand.

VI.

And I gat wealthy in this same world's wealth,
    And felt soft favours spread beneath my feet,
And watched my earlier scorners, as by stealth,

Turn to be made my friends : (as 'twas most meet,

    Seeing 'twas known of me, no common heat

Can melt fine ore).   And here, upon my breast,

    I wore such things as Emperors do greet ;

And all the cities from the east to west

Were little glories 'neath me ;—He, my crown, the best.

VII.

Why, then, am I left thus lonely with the dead ?—

    No friendly hand to hold my palsied palm ?—

To share with me the watching of his bed,

    Nor soothe my soul with what would be my

        balm :—

    A quick'ning physic fraught with no bitter qualm :

Tuning sweet virtues that in him were stored

    And hoarded up, like high thoughts in a psalm ?—

If mine are subject-friends, and I their Lord,

It is my pencil scares them—not my edgeless sword.

VIII.

Then, if I have that Cato-part in me !—

    Splendid restraint and patience over grief ;—

Let my stern brush retrace, though painfully,

His pale perdition for my lone relief.

Thus He shall live when to the golden sheaf

All ours is gathered ; and his deathlessness

Shall mock the triumph of Life's trenchant thief,

Smiling in manhood ; and my dire distress

Will thus memorialize my former blissfulness.

IX.

Even as the patriarch, when he raised his knife

In pent-up anguish over his sweet son,

And looked on Woe's worst horror without strife,

Believing God's true justice must be done,

Though a dread deed should darken-through the

sun ;—

Or as on high, Himself, the glorious God,

Marked wondering the scarlet passion run

From the Redeemer's side down to the sod,

Which, for the whole world's sake, in sorrow soft He

trod ;—

X.

So will I dauntless scatter the veil of Death,

Though my beloved's body lies behind ;

And limn the kingdom of his sweet life's breath,
 And throne the soul which Death hath tried to
  bind.
 And every wreath of thought his lips entwined
Shall shine in life-like radiance, as he wore
 Its heart-enchanting wonder,—ere the wind
That seems to freeze my veins unto their core,
Had driven these smitten leaflets through Death's
 chamber-door.

VENICE, *4th Nov.*, 1879.

SOUVENIR.

ONE sole sweet thing of the Earth is this.
    It is no creed to be bought or sold ;
It is no gift for a priest to kiss ;
    Only a little dead gold.

Like an infant asleep in its faery cot,
    Folded away from the days of old ;—
Blissful to look upon ; yet, God wot !—
    Only a little dead gold !

As the curled bright shape of a crosier-frond,
    That glittereth green from the mellow mould ;—
Yet kindling a passion than April more fond ;—
    Is this little dead gold !

Like a virgin cloud in the noontide sun,
    That flowers the air with shades manifold ;—
So floats o'er my heart till my day be done,
    This little dead gold !

Like music that waves and wanes as it moves,
  It hints of high things that will never be told ;
Vague visions are all that its mystery proves,—
    This little dead gold !

Yet of all sweet things that the seasons bring ;
  Of all bright things that a man can behold ;
There is to my soul no sweet, bright thing
    So dear as this little dead gold.

AFTER A SPRING-STORM.

SCATTERED twigs upon the lawn,
Hewn from the boughs 'twixt night and dawn ;
Broken buds in the sunlight pale,
Mourned of linnet and yaffingale.

    " Winter with his cruel knife
    Tried to sever out our life ;
    Failing this, he would us kill
    With freezing up each little rill
    That flowed out so sweet and free
    From our stately mother-tree ;—
    Till benumbed we grew asleep,
    Careless how our life to keep :
    Then we dreamed of the wind of Love
    Wafting the song of the turtle-dove ;
    And below us we saw the spring
    Rise like snow-flowers in a ring ;
    And like a sweet we cannot name,
    The violet's wild odour came ;

And a little amorous beam,

Breaking with rapture our bright dream,

Woke us to Hope : but here we lie,

Full of despair and like to die,—

Good Lady, lift us pitifully."

IDYLL.

I.

OFT from our sea-lad's lips come forth
Queer stories of the cloudy north ;
Where Winter, tyrant, sternly binds
Earth's beauty with heart-biting winds.
All frozen stiff, the folded shrouds ;
   And hopelessly doth lour the sky ;—
So that, saith He, "perpetual clouds
   Make the scarce sun a mockery."

II.

Ah ! happy then that I should live
Where God such store of good doth give,
That Summer sees her face of glee
Visaged on the tideless sea ;—
Where the high sweet-fruited pine
Sceptres each headland haunt divine ;—
And where heaven's bosom brightly heaves
With eternal olive-leaves ;—

And at my feet, through fadeless hours,

(Shaded by vine leaves from the glare,)

Innumerous breath-stealing flowers,

Hold rainbow-court upon the air.

III.

One certain truth to me this brings

Amidst uncertain other things :—

I live out my little lease

In the sweets of health and peace ;

Nor shall I quit this vale of years

With eye-lids quite unfilled with tears,

Unless these powers (and who can tell

What kind of death is his to die ?)—

Shall make me by their magic spell

Pass from it all unwittingly !

SORRENTO, 29 *Dec.*, 1879.

THE FIRE-FLY.

I.

WHAT is the moonlight
To thee,—or the sunlight ?—
Thou art a meteor
Unhindered by limits
Of tyrannous orbits.
Sorrow-hued darkness,—
Blinding to mortals,—
Illumines thy jewel :—
Seems made for thy glory
Fair Elfin for thee !

II.

Confusing thy slayers
With effortless splendour,
Astray they are blund'ring,
Like the old Cyclops,
Reft of clear vision.

Yet to the traveller
Thy favour is endless ;—
Aiding and lighting
Through the lone forest :
And ever he blesses,
And bears thee the praise !

THE FLYING-FISH.

OUT of the billow
Gleaming with moonlight,
Cleaving the sea-wind,
On swallow-like pinions
Thou flyest.   Below thee,—
Hard enemies press thee,—
Monsters pursue thee :
Then breathing the evening—
The balm of the ocean,
Sea-mews are labouring
There to destroy thee !
Grace and thy beauty
Though blissful and godlike,
Bring thee to ruin.
Escape is existence.

THE HALLOWED SPOT.

HERE is a deep glen where the sea looks in.
   Its sheer sides wave with fern as the breezes urge :
   Tall pines peer down from on its topmost verge :
And starry orange-gardens gleam within.
But wouldst thou gaze up yonder where the smoke
   Curls, like an infant's arms, above ;—
Nestles the cot there sweetly where awoke
      My own dear Love!

JOY-FLOWER.

SWEETEST Pleasure blooms around us.
  If with bountiful restraint
We would pluck its fairest blossoms ;—
  Suchwise it would never faint !

Should it languish for an hour :—
  Yielding no brilliant fruit :
Still there were joy within the flower,
  So life were in the root.

BEFORE THE SEA.

LIFT up thine eyes, my song ; look free
Over the glad green fields of the sea.
The sea-grass ripples ; the sun-fire shakes,—
Like those wide, lily-woven lakes,
Where the summer moonbeams strew
Lightnings o'er the chaliced dew.

The sea is as an April grove,
Where every breath is fraught with Love :
She is our mother, from all harms
We gather unto her mild white arms.
And when the wolvish winds of Death
Raven madly for our breath ;
Her fingers are as a million swords
That smite for us the famished hordes.
Her voice is as the thunder's roar,
Trembling through the vasty shore :—
Until her fiery soul hath slain
The murderous mad hurricane.

And then the rosy-smiling west
Brightens her beautiful chafed breast ;
And on her hair, broke from its tire,
Blushes his tremulous desire.
While her virgins, watch are keeping
Round our infinite soft sleeping,
Where the choral underbreath
Of the charmed sea, murmureth.

O sea, our mother ! O magic sea !
All things gather unto Thee.
In thy marvellous soft smile
All things sweetly reconcile.
From thy bosom, soft as dove,
Swelled with bright electric Love,
Man has drunk the sacred fire
In his riotous desire :—
Raptured at delight so rare,
Trembling like a strucken lyre,
Smitten with death-notes passing fair.
I have seen his lips turn white
With ineffable delight,
And a faint sweet smile arise

From his beautiful strange eyes,
When thy wine, like Love's own dart,
Wafted Elysium through his heart :
When thy murmurous voice was hushed,
And thy tremulous bright fingers rushed
In delirious, keen shocks
Through his cool, close-clinging locks ;
And all around his limbs of snow
Thy body's soft resplendent glow
Brake into fountainous bright spray,
Like sudden stars at break of day.

O sea, their mother ! O magic sea !
All things hasten unto Thee.
I have watched a summer flower
Stream to thy eternity :
And the mild, soft mountain-shower
Move toward thee lovingly,
Till lost, as is a sunward dove,
In thy immensity of Love.
Even the mighty cliffs that stand,
Lean sweetly down at Thy command :—
Yea ! e'en the haughtiest empires bow

At thy wrathsome jealous brow.
I have seen thee spin to death
The moth-like cloud that mocked thy breath.
Thou hast thy lightning as thy smiles;
And thy sweetly-woven wiles
Drew our dearest unto thee!

O sea, my mother! O magic sea!
I dare not gaze upon thee long.
I dread to hear thy glad sweet song.
The very thought of thy controul
Smites a soft terror to my soul.
Yea! and God knows what thou hast ta'en,
Thou wilt never give again.
Therefore when my daystar falls,
Take me too to thy dreamland halls.

THE NIGHT COMES.

I.

LEAVING the scenes that through Him shone,
Sinks the fadeless God alone :
　　Where the darkening sea, his mantle,—hides ;
And where his crimson wings have flown,
　　With glittering seraphs at her sides,
　　The grey-eyed Evening glides
To His lost throne !

II.

And, like a dawnlit dewy fleece,
Myriads of stars for sweet release
　　Break into choral glimmerings ;
And with sweet voice, divine increase
　　Of Love, Night on her fragrant wings
　　To Lovers wise and faithful, brings ;—
With tender Peace !

BOCCACCIO AT VIRGIL'S TOMB.

OUT at last from sunny, mendicant Naples!
Let me stand and breathe the blue sweet heaven ;—
Fresh from yon sea that darkens back its love!
I, Boccaccio, what should I do in Naples?
Is there a northern Earl more free than me
When inly my soul wanders and delights?
Why, here, beneath my feet, adown the rocks,
The rippling tiny fern is freely glad,
And mimics the far waters over there,
Even as a child that spreads its starry palms
Upon the strings a master touches too,
Just as the heavenly spirit it inspires,
Because the earth has yet baptized it not
With the chill fount of sin's profundity!
The very ilex boughs, the frosted olive,
The mounded pines that make the tempest moan :
That burn their sullen smiles towards the sun,—
Are as mere prisoners rusting in dull chains

Beside the glory of my soul that stands here !
And here like spirits fair of earth's first spring,
The wings of Beauty's self flit by, inspired !

And yet no villain in his filthy cell ;
No moth to whom a flame brought worse than Death ;
No bird that pines bereft his native food :
Is hindered in his yearning, as am I !

The dust of Maro lies within yon tomb.
It was not Death that made a temple there :
It is the pledge-spot where the angels met,
And on their golden wings encrossed, upbore him
To that fair other place where glorious God
Smiled, and the silver stars of morning sang !
And what am I, Giovanni ?   What am I ?
The plodding, drudging, honest craven clerks,
That are the silver in their master's pocket,
Among whom I am but as a small stray copper,—
Tell me I am a dreamer : and with their pens,
And thin sharp noses, grieve at my additions !
" Better," say they, " you wrote your Lady's dreams
Than these accounts : for giving you them means

Many a candle for us.   We do believe
Your nights are spent among those Latin poets
And dreams exhaust you not of what you think :
Therefore an office is not fit for you."
Then, in the freedom that my evenings give,—
Ere the dull work looms yet upon the morn,—
Sweet gentle eyes that glitter to my longing,
Breaking to smiles—like water thrown on water,—
Tell me too that I dream.   But what of this?
Surely if I, beneath each silent flower ;
Beneath the mountains, in the sun, the wind,
And in all objects that the light reveals
Fancy I see a deep Divinity,—
Imagine mirrors that reflect God's heart :
Omnipotent and all-pervading Beauty !
So that my soul fires with the thought of it,
And passion flames my breath to mention it.
Surely my dreams might lift my life and theirs.
Their scoffs, without my will, like treacherous hounds,
Will turn upon themselves.   How should they know ?
Poor souls ! that never once laughed healthily,
But live behind a daubed screen called Life,
And never see true Beauty nor themselves;—

But all things in a sick, distorting mirror!
How should they know?—But yet I, having seen,
How can I dare desire that glorious name,—
Poet?—a name that woos the tenderest tongue!
Poet!—that holds the whole world's history!
Poet!—that vessel of God's living fire!
Wherein all passion, beauty, and delight
Streak the uprising everlasting flame;
But now defamed by every ribald singer,—
Blasphemed, degraded: held in all men's sight
A thing almost unworthy spitting on:—
A synonym for sin: a red-haired vice
That cannot rise above the jealous lust
Of angry beasts.   How should one hold the same?
Ah! we had glowing Dante! loved him not!
His splendid Anger would not burn his Florence:—
" For," said he, " Peradventure there are five!"
And his heart's echo cried: " Behold, I save!"
But he foresaw that Rage reburns herself:—
Who would have made him, like a puppet-show,
Upon a gala-day.

     And there, thou tomb:
Whence reverent hands have stripped the holy laurel:

Thou hast the dust immortal Mantua bore ;
Her walls reverberated that true pang
That winged the singing Virgil into light.
Here, all the loving flowers and seasons turn :
Even as in his verse, the keys of passion
Modulate their glorious Antiphones
Through rests more potent than the notes that bring
   them !

O Muse, despise me not !   In thy last court
The merest slave,—I will be true to thee !
And though the work be menial, scoffed, derided,—
I will not ask of thee a laurel-crown :
But give me merely sweet sincerity,
And humbly let me shine in days to come !

CRUEL AMOR.

I.

SWIFT, too swift, to another land!—
  Since at home I could not stay more.
Ah! that he could feel my hand,—
  That little impish Elf, called Amor!

II.

When new scenes do most delight me,—
  Straight he brings her to my vision :—
Bids e'en memory bespite me :—
  Then He flies in glib derision!

KING AND COUNTESS.

A BALLAD.

I.

" Tush, child! our race were sore assoiled
    Were ye wed to such a knight;
Well, too, I wis your dower is spoiled,
    If to him your troth be plight."

II.

" Nay, Aunt, if kind and true, her knight,
    What more should Lady seek?—
There lives not one so brave and bright."
    A tear shone down her cheek.

III.

Like a bird to its cosy nest,
Rosalie has flown to rest;
And all the castle's charmèd might
Silverly sleeps in the clear moonlight.

Only the Countess, in her chair
   By the great hall-fire, agleam :
Like a lioness in her lair,
   Heavily breathes her savage dream.

IV.

Why starts sweet Rosalie before
The broken light on her chamber floor ?
" It is his form ! his face it is."
Full soon return they kiss for kiss.

V.

He holds her white in his steely arm :
She quivers (for steel has a tang of alarm).
   But it is not for maidenly fear of sin
     She entreats him swiftly to go :—
   " Should our fierce guard the ladder win,
     Your blood, my Sweet, would flow."

VI.

What sound is it now that troubles his ears ?
Why widen her lids as with fluctuant tears ?—

O

'Tis the clank of the sentinel halberdiers,
As they pass through the portal and lower their
    spears.—
     " Alas ! my heart's true lady, see ;
       Their pikes gleam through the place :
     Wildly they glare on thee and me :—
       (*Aside.*) Hurl treasons at my face !
     Let me go down, nor fear to die,
       Would Death thee benefit !—
     Soldiers, the man who scorns to fly
       Should have good grace of it."

VII.

But, with bared swords and daggers bright,
    They waited his knightly foot to earth.

" What curs are ye whose mongrel might
    Thinks to daunt a soul of worth ?"

VIII.

When the moonlight lit his face,
It seemed as though some magic grace
    Did charm them from their ire ;

Upright he stood amid the band—
One alone of them raised his hand ;
   But quenched his fierce desire.

IX.

In vengeful zeal the Countess comes !
   " At last for bars and locks,
I've caught the beast that nightly roams
   To vex my goose—Sir Fox.
What now, ye caitives, shrinking there !
   At once his vile neck wring !"
" My Lady, say, how shall we dare ?"
   " Strike *him* !"—" It is the King !"

HATEM AND THE SULTAN.

I.

HIGH on his emerald throne of state
Mighty Zoheir proudly sate ;
The balmy gale blew through the doors
Upon him there and his councillors ;
To that sagely-frowning throng
It bore a soft and glorious song,
That mounted high with a noble name :
" Hatem the Bounteous" was the same ;
And it burnt the king like a thunder-flame.

II.

Envy smote him e'en to blindness,
 Though he smiled full pleasantly :
" What is Hatem, that his kindness
 Needs your mean emblazonry ?
Oft I've seen my royal father
 Rally Hatem with a frown !
Hold ye : for ourself I'll rather
 Test this worthy's wide renown."

III.

Thus he spake.   None dared prolong
The plenteous burthen of the song ;
But softly whispered each to each.
Again (but softlier) went his speech.—

IV.

" He has one dark steed—the glory of his beautiful
domain :
For that steed, bold Abdel Rahman, beg, and turn not
back in vain.
Should he yield the peerless courser, be it our Imperial
whim—
We will surfeit him with treasure, then restore the
steed to him."

V.

So the Vizier featly travelled till he greeted fields of
light,
Till, before his glittering palace, Hatem welcomed
him that night.
All its courts rang sweet with music, like the woods of
early Spring ;
Nor was spared no lordly lavish for his utmost
honouring.

VI.

But when dewy morn had risen to refresh each wearied
    guest,
Tenderly Hatem pressed each grateful kinsman to his
    gentle breast.

But some shrunk to silent trembling,
Looking vexed, e'en though dissembling.
Hatem : " Not for nought a monarch greeteth :—
    Let me know my Sultan's need."
Others for shame in both cheeks burned,
Marvelling what would be returned.
But the Vizier soft, yet gravely,
Spake his heartless mission bravely :—
" Master, our mighty lord entreateth
    For the Morning-Star—your Steed."

VII.

First a tear escaped him ; turning,
    For a breath he spake no word ;
Then, with chastened passion burning,
    Forth his voice fell, like a sword :—

" Tell him, far my flocks were feeding
  When your suite made my domain ;
And for their last night's good-speeding
  That—my Joy—was slain."

HATEM AND THE KING OF YEMEN.

Comp: Decam: Tenth Day: Nov: III.

" TO be peerless in our bounty is the glory of our
　　race;
So in this, I, King of Yemen, bear no rival to my face.
How long in my Royal palace will ye thus to heart-
　　ache give
Fresher pang?—Say, why is Hatem, such-wise foe—
　　let free to live?"

I.

Soon as those words went through the hall,
Great fear and pity came on all:
Many a tear from Lady fell,
Pitying one all loved so well.
Was it in sooth, or cruel sport?
A gloomy henchman left the court—
Nedim—famous (for he speeds
Tyranny's most fell misdeeds).

II.

Out of the golden gate he went :
His path toward the desert bent :
Nor reined he once his cursed steed
To list soft bribes to stay the deed.
Two toilsome days alone he hied :
On the third his courser died.
Storms of sand half-closed his eyes,
And sand-reflected heat, and flies.

Many a sorry day of wand'ring wearied out each
    labouring limb,
Ere he met the hand of Pity softly held to welcome
    him.—
" Enter thou our mansion cheering—there is ample
    space for all :
Safely with me trust thy purpose, that my aid may
    fitly fall.
(*Aside.*) " E'en though dire I dare not hide it from a
    friend so mild and kind,
I was sent to search out Hatem, and to slay him when
    I find."

" Smite, then, quickly !" cried the stranger, " strike
    while sweet occasion bends,
And, by slaying him this instant, spite the vengeance
    of his friends.
I am Hatem ! You my guest are in the hour of sore
    distress ;
Further still my heart is open—would you drain its
    sinfulness ?"

    But self-hate and sudden shame
    Nedim's craven heart o'ercame ;
    As a meteor falleth fleet,
    He fell and sobbed at Hatem's feet.

Then with cheer and costly treasure in resplendent
    equipage,
Hatem sent him to his master. But the King fell dead
    of rage.

THE TREE-GOD.

I.

BROKEN shadows wild and free
   O'er the western strand are stealing :
   Gentle Hatem humbly kneeling
Worships at the God-dwelt tree.
All the God-gifts glow with sunlight
   Like the tears upon his eyes :
He has lost e'en her—the one light
   Of his child-home's paradise.

II.

" Who was like thee, O my sister ?—
   Was there a flower in all our land ?—
I marvel not old Death hath kissed her,
   Raptured at her sweet white hand !—
Yet, O God !"—(He prays the beech-tree)—
   " Leave me not behind her long.
By my sorrow I beseech thee :—
   By the sorrow of my song."

III.

Though the darkness of distress
Maketh all things beautiless,
Yet a glittering web hath bound him :—
Yea, a fire divine hath found him :—
Sweet relief for loneliness!

IV.

Fair Zuleika, having seen him,
  Would her own dark grief disguise :—
Lifts her silken vest to screen him ;—
  (As it were to dry her eyes.)
Then upon the stilly air,
In the beauty of despair,
To the Tree-God lifts her prayer.—

V.

" Take away my spirit, Father,
  To thy palace in high Heaven :
Any death I'd woo me, rather
  Than on earth be friendless driven."

VI.

Seeing her in Grief's prostration,
   Sorrow lightened : Joy oppressed :
One might, through his cheek's elation,
   See the God worked in his breast.
In her ears his soul is singing
   Comfort and youth's sympathy ;
While the starlit woods are ringing
   With the night-bird plaintively.

VII.

Gently then he raised her to him :
   Drew her bosom to his heart :—
Knew her passion ere she knew him :—
   Vowed their lives should never part.—
Touched the glistening tear-drops from her,
   As a bee from flower sips ;—
Like the breeze of early summer,
   Took the sweetness from her lips.

VIII.

Slowly then through woodland shadows,—
   His lithe arm around her waist—

Wend they ; then o'er the balmy meadows,
  Like twin flowerets interlaced.
Hope within them burning brightly,
  Heaven beholds in every star ;
While a mocking laughter lightly
  From the Tree-God comes afar !

THE LEGEND OF THE KINGFISHER.

And like the Halcyon's birth
Be thine to bring a calm upon the shore !
CHAPMAN, *Byron's Tragedy.*

Lo the dark-eyed beautiful Amphitrite
Lonely threads her ivory-pillared temple,
Smiling 'neath the sapphirine sky of Corinth,
    Daughter of Tethys.
All the grave soft song of her early worship
Waxes and wanes no longer in her lone hearing ;
But the drear despairfully moaning plaint of
    Fatherless daughters,
Falling on her silk-enstrung ears of silver :—
(Even as on Æolian harps the night-wind
Smiting, breatheth mystic and mendless sorrow,)—
    Turns her to Pity.
Straight she speeds where winelike the sun is pouring
Into her glowing golden-winged cup of omen,
Where the fervent virginal grief-white faces
    Seem to entreat her.

Then with sudden wonder of two-fold wisdom
Waving o'er the chalice her flower-wove sceptre
Turns the tearful dolorous kneeling maidens
    Into gay Halcyons.
So that sailors, curbed of her crowned lord Neptune,
Seeing seaward Iris-like flying birdlets,
May full surely speed on their doubtful passage,
    Flouting the roadstead.
Aye! and the wary merchant may draft his spices :
And that the long-gone traveller turn him homeward,
And the loved poet may in the lap of Ocean
    Rest from his ardour!

THE PROPHET'S HARVEST.

ABROAD on the land
Went beautiful Summer.
The fields grew golden.
They waved like the ocean
When the glad Sungod
Smiles through the braided
Locks of a tempest.
Stormwind and shower
Crushed them and vexed them.
Ah! but the Day-king
Lifted and strengthened !—
Watched them reviving
Gracefully heavenwards :
Till, in their glory,
They fill the horizon.—
No single vision
Can see to the end of it :
And soon will be near us

The time of the shearing.
All the world's nations
Will smile at its splendour :
And winter no longer
Will frown with affliction !

SPRING IN WINTER.

THE flowers are gone from the Earth.
　　The trees are utterly bare ;
And faded the voices of mirth,
　　And all that was joyous and fair.

II.

Dear Love, as I pass down the street,
　　Each face seems pale and sad.
In my face, only, they greet
　　A spirit unfadingly glad !

CHISWICK PRESS:—CHARLES WHITTINGHAM AND CO.,
TOOKS COURT, CHANCERY LANE.

www.ingramcontent.com/pod-product-compliance
Lightning Source LLC
Chambersburg PA
CBHW030124030726
47498CB00007B/2541